7.46

LITTLE SHOP
OF HAMSTERS

GOOSEBUMPS HorrorLand™
ALL-NEW! ALL-TERRIFYING!
Also Available from Scholastic Audio Books

RIDE FOR YOUR LIFE!

THE VIDEO GAME
From Scholastic Interactive

GET GOOSEBUMPS PHOTOSHOCK FOR YOUR
iPhone™ OR iPod touch®

GOOSEBUMPS®
NOW WITH BONUS FEATURES!
LOOK IN THE BACK OF THE BOOK
FOR EXCLUSIVE AUTHOR INTERVIEWS AND MORE.

NIGHT OF THE LIVING DUMMY
DEEP TROUBLE
MONSTER BLOOD
THE HAUNTED MASK
ONE DAY AT HORRORLAND
THE CURSE OF THE MUMMY'S TOMB
BE CAREFUL WHAT YOU WISH FOR
SAY CHEESE AND DIE!
THE HORROR AT CAMP JELLYJAM
HOW I GOT MY SHRUNKEN HEAD
WEREWOLF OF FEVER SWAMP
A NIGHT IN TERROR TOWER
WELCOME TO DEAD HOUSE
WELCOME TO CAMP NIGHTMARE
GHOST BEACH

GET MORE
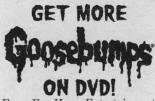
ON DVD!
From Fox Home Entertainment

ATTACK OF THE JACK-O-LANTERNS
THE HEADLESS GHOST
MONSTER BLOOD
A NIGHT IN TERROR TOWER
ONE DAY AT HORRORLAND
RETURN OF THE MUMMY
THE SCARECROW WALKS AT MIDNIGHT

LITTLE SHOP OF HAMSTERS

R.L. STINE

SCHOLASTIC INC.
New York Toronto London Auckland
Sydney Mexico City New Delhi Hong Kong

ISBN 978-0-545-16195-4

Goosebumps book series created by Parachute Press, Inc.

12 11 10 9 8 7 6 5 4 3 2 1   10 11 12 13 14 15/0

Printed in the U.S.A.   40
First printing, March 2010

MEET JONATHAN CHILLER . . .

He owns Chiller House, the HorrorLand gift shop. Sometimes he doesn't let kids pay for their souvenirs. Chiller tells them, "You can pay me *next time.*"

What does he mean by *next time*? What is Chiller's big plan?

Go ahead — the gates are opening. Enter HorrorLand. This time you might be permitted to leave . . . but for how long? Jonathan Chiller is waiting — to make sure you TAKE A LITTLE HORROR HOME WITH YOU!

PART ONE

1

Let me start out by saying that I love animals. And I'm desperate to have a pet of my own.

I'm so desperate, I even enjoyed petting the werewolves in the Werewolf Petting Zoo at HorrorLand Theme Park.

Yes, there is a big pen outside Werewolf Village. You go inside, and you can pet the werewolves, rub their bellies, and scratch their furry backs.

A big sign says: JUST DON'T PUT YOUR HAND IN THEIR MOUTHS.

Pretty good advice.

Should I back up and tell you who I am and stuff like that? Sometimes, I get so *psyched* about animals I forget to do anything else.

My name is Sam Waters. I'm twelve, and so is my friend Lexi Blake. Lexi and I spent a week at HorrorLand, and we had some good, scary fun. Especially since our parents let us wander off on our own.

Lexi is tall and blond and kind of chirpy and giggly and *very* enthusiastic. I guess she comes on a little strong, but I'm used to her. We've been friends since we were three.

I'm not exactly the quiet type, either. My parents say that sometimes when Lexi and I get together, we're like chattering magpies. I've never seen a magpie, so I don't really know what they are talking about. I keep meaning to Google *magpies*. Maybe they make good pets.

I'm shorter than Lexi. Actually, I'm one of the shortest guys in the sixth grade. But I could still have a growth spurt, right?

I have short black hair and dark eyes, and my two front teeth poke out a little when I smile, just like my little brother, Noah.

Bunny teeth, Dad calls them. And then I always say, "Could I have a bunny for a pet?" He's so sick of me asking, he usually doesn't even answer. Just makes a groaning noise.

Anyway, it was a hot, sunny summer afternoon. Lexi and I walked out of the Werewolf Petting Zoo into the crowded park.

"Those werewolves were totally gross," Lexi said, wiping her hands on the sides of her dark green shorts. "Their fur was sticky, like they were sweating or something."

"I don't think wolves sweat," I said. "I think the bristles on their fur feel sticky because — HEY!"

4

Lexi pulled me out of the way of a rolling food cart. The side of the cart said: FAST FOOD. A green-and-purple Horror was chasing after it.

"They couldn't be real werewolves," Lexi said. "But they didn't look like regular wolves — did they?"

"They had human eyes," I said. "I mean . . . the way those werewolves looked at us. Like they were smarter than animals. And their fangs were longer than wolf fangs."

Lexi shivered. "You're creeping me out, Sam." She crinkled up her face. "They sure *smelled* like animals. Yuck. I can't get the smell out of my nose. They stunk!"

I pinched my nose. "Are you sure it was the werewolves?"

She grabbed the park map from my hand and smacked me on the shoulder with it. We wrestled around a little.

"Are you hungry?" she asked. "I'm hungry. Hungry enough to bite a werewolf!"

She snapped her teeth at me a few times. I had to push her away. "Down, girl! Down!"

I grabbed the map away from her. "Let's see where we are. There's probably a restaurant somewhere. . . ."

I unfolded the map and raised it to my face. The sun was so bright, I needed to squint to read it.

"Let me help," Lexi said. She tugged at the

map — too hard — and ripped it in half. She burst out laughing. "Hey — I don't know my own strength!"

"Please don't help me," I groaned. "You're always trying to help me."

"What's the big deal, Sam?" she said. "You read your half and I'll read my half."

"We don't have to read the map," I told her. I pointed. "Look. That's a little restaurant right there."

We crossed the wide path and peeked into the open door. It was a lunch-counter place. Round red stools in front of a long yellow counter.

I read the sign beside the door. THE SPEAR-IT CAFÉ: IF YOU CAN SPEAR IT, YOU CAN EAT IT!

"Huh?" I read the sign again. "What does *that* mean? This doesn't sound too good."

"I don't care," Lexi said. She grabbed me around the waist and pushed me inside. "I'm starving. We're eating here."

I stumbled into the little restaurant. We took seats at the end of the counter.

And that's when all the trouble began.

"Why are we the only ones here?" I asked Lexi.

She picked up a plastic menu from the counter. "That's good," she said. "We'll get our food faster."

I picked up the fork in front of me. It had something green and disgusting — like a booger — stuck to it. A greasy, smoky smell came from the kitchen behind the counter.

I could hear someone humming back there. And through the small window, I saw a man in a white chef's hat waving a metal spatula in the air.

"Weird menu," Lexi muttered.

The cook stepped out from the kitchen. He pulled off the chef's hat. He was bald and red-faced and sweaty. His blue eyes rolled around in his head like loose marbles. "Hey," he said. "Lunchtime, huh?"

He pulled a wad of green bubble gum from his mouth and stuck it behind his ear. Then he wiped his pudgy hands on the front of his grease-stained apron.

"Welcome. Welcome," he said. He had a gruff, hoarse voice. He brushed a dead fly off the counter. "Welcome, guys. I'm Chef Belcher."

Belcher? I said to myself.

"And don't make any jokes about my name," he said. "I don't think it's funny." He wiped his sweaty bald head with one hand. "Need any help with the menu?"

"Well . . ." I glanced over Lexi's shoulder at her menu. "Do you have —"

"The fried snot sandwich really isn't as bad as it sounds," Chef Belcher said. "It's not really snot — it's fish mucus."

"That's *sick*," Lexi whispered.

"The soup of the day is Badger Tongue," Belcher said.

I shifted my weight on the stool. "You're joking, right?" I said.

Belcher leaned close to me. I could see the big droplets of sweat on his red forehead. "Try the soup," he rasped. "See if I'm joking."

"I'll have a grilled cheese sandwich," Lexi said.

"Good choice," Belcher replied. "I made the cheese myself. Between my toes. Ha-ha."

He turned to me. "Have you ever tried sheep liver served really rare?"

8

My stomach lurched. I almost gagged. My eyes scanned the menu. "I'll have the fried shrimp basket."

Belcher nodded. He pulled the bubble gum from behind his ear and shoved it back into his mouth. Then he disappeared into the kitchen.

"Awesome restaurant," Lexi said.

We both laughed.

"What do you want to do after lunch?" I asked.

"Some rides," she said. "Where's that underground ride? It's like a roller coaster, only it goes straight down? I think it's called the R.I.P.P.E.R. Dipper." I studied the map. "It's not on my half," I said. "Do you want to do the Doom Slide again? That was kind of scary."

"No repeats," she said. "We have only one more day here."

"Well, we haven't done The Bottomless Canoe Ride," I said, gazing at the torn map.

She shook her head. "I don't have my bathing suit on. I don't want to get wet."

We were still trying to decide what to do next when Chef Belcher returned from the kitchen. He plopped our food down in front of us. "Enjoy," he said. "And don't worry. I keep a stomach pump in the back."

The warm aroma rose up from the basket

in front of me. I tried a few French fries. Not bad. Then I looked down at the fried shrimp.

"Whoa!" I let out a cry. "These shrimp look weird!"

They were shaped like worms. But they seemed to have fluttery wings at one end.

I picked one up. It wriggled in my hand. I dropped it back into the basket.

"It's ALIVE!" I cried. "It's MOVING!"

Lexi set her sandwich down and leaned over my shrimp basket. "Yeah. They're definitely moving," she said. "I guess that's what the sign means, Sam. The Spear-It Café. You're supposed to *spear* the shrimp!"

"No way!" I cried. "I can't eat this. I —"

I gasped as a shrimp jumped out of the basket onto the back of my hand. It prickled.

"Hey!" I could feel it digging into my skin.

Another shrimp wriggled over the side of the basket and dropped onto the lunch counter. Then it jumped onto my wrist.

I swung my arm hard. But the weird shrimp dug into my skin and didn't let go. A third shrimp jumped onto my hand. And they all began to climb up my arm.

I slapped my arm against the counter. I tried to brush the shrimp off with my other hand.

But they clung to my skin. Two more jumped

onto me. They climbed my arm. And they started to make loud sucking noises.

Like leeches!

My arm itched and tingled and throbbed.

"Help me!" I shouted. "Hey — help me! My food — it's *eating* me!"

"Let me help!" Lexi cried. She grabbed my arm and pulled it toward her.

"OWWWW!" I let out a scream. "You're breaking my arm! It doesn't bend that way!"

"Sam! I'm sorry." She wrapped her fingers around a shrimp and tugged it hard.

I let out another scream.

"Stop! It's clamped on tight. You're pulling my *skin* off! Please — stop helping me!"

"Oooh, sick! Sam — your arm — it's totally covered!" Lexi cried.

"They're sucking my BLOOD!" I screamed.

Chef Belcher stomped out from the kitchen. "What's the problem here?" he growled. "You don't like my shrimp?"

I started to swing my arm frantically back and forth. They were biting . . . digging into my skin. My arm tingled and throbbed.

"Get them OFF me!" I screamed. "Get them OFF!"

Belcher squinted at the swarm of wormlike shrimps on my arm. "I know what you need," he said calmly. "A little hot sauce."

He grabbed a slender red bottle off the counter. Pulled off the cap and began to pour a thick red liquid over my arm.

SSSSSSSSSS.

It made a sizzling sound.

I gasped again.

Was that my *skin* burning off?

I jumped off the stool. The sizzle grew louder as Belcher poured on more hot sauce. Pumping the bottle up and down, he emptied the sauce over my arm.

As I stared in horror, the wormy creatures began to drop off. They fell in clumps onto the counter and lay on their backs without moving. Then the creatures curled into tiny balls.

Belcher grinned. "That's good hot sauce!" he exclaimed. He raised the bottle to his lips and drank some.

My chest was heaving. I was panting hard.

I grabbed a bunch of napkins off the counter and frantically wiped off my arm.

Lexi stared down at the tiny balled-up creatures. "Ohhh, gross," she moaned.

She pulled my other arm. "Hurry, Sam! Let's get out of here!"

Still wiping the red sauce off my tingling

arm, I turned and ran after Lexi to the open door.

"Wait! Come back!" Belcher yelled from behind the counter. "Come back! You've won a free dessert!"

4

We didn't stop. We hurtled out into the sunlight.

"Wait!" Belcher called. "Come back! It was all a joke! *Everything* is a joke in HorrorLand!"

Lexi and I raced through the crowds. I was so desperate to get away, I *leaped* over a baby stroller and kept running. The mother shouted at me angrily.

Lexi and I turned a corner and found ourselves facing a row of small shops. Two little boys stepped out of a mask store, wearing ugly monster masks. People were lined up at a food cart to buy Frozen Chocolate-Covered Chihuahuas on a Stick.

"Those can't be real Chihuahuas," Lexi said as we finally slowed to a walk. She bent down, grabbed her knees, and struggled to catch her breath. "Maybe those leech creatures weren't real, either."

I rubbed my arm. *They sure felt real,* I thought. *Or was it all just HorrorLand special effects?*

I turned around. We were standing in front of a souvenir store. The front window was jammed with all kinds of funny, creepy gifts.

I saw a full-size mummy head resting on a wooden box. The eyes glowed bright red. A skeleton marionette danced behind it. A giant egg was cracked open. I saw a green hand reaching out from inside the shell.

I read the sign above the door: CHILLER HOUSE.

"Cool," I said. The door made a squeaky creaking noise as I pulled it open. Lexi and I stepped inside.

The store was dimly lit. Shelves piled high with souvenirs ran from floor to ceiling. We squeezed down the narrow aisles, checking everything out. I saw a very real-looking squirting rattlesnake . . . a drawer of "Human Fingers" . . . a monkey-head key chain.

Lexi picked up a sweet-looking baby doll with blue eyes and curly blond hair. When she picked the doll up, the face changed until it looked like an ugly dried-up prune — and it opened its mouth in a deafening screech.

Lexi jumped in surprise — and dropped the doll back onto the shelf.

I turned to the front counter. "Does anyone work here?" I called.

A man stepped out from behind a display

16

case. I blinked a few times. He looked very old-fashioned. Like out of a history book or something.

He was big and nearly bald. He looked a lot like Benjamin Franklin.

He had little square eyeglasses perched low on his long, pointed nose. His bushy white eyebrows hung over his pale blue eyes. His scraggly gray hair was swept straight back on his broad pink forehead.

He wore a stiff-looking dark suit with a vest under the jacket, a ruffly white shirt, and a floppy black bow tie.

"Hello. Welcome to Chiller House," he said. He had a croaky old man's voice. I saw a gold tooth gleam in the side of his mouth. "My name is Jonathan Chiller."

As he rubbed his hands together, I saw a sparkly blue-jeweled ring on one of his long, slender fingers.

Chiller took a few steps toward us. He walked slowly with a slight limp. "Where did you two come from?" he asked.

"The Spear-It Café," I said.

He grinned. "I hope you didn't order the shrimp. It's *terrible!*"

Jonathan Chiller began pulling items off the shelves to show to us. "You might like this," he said. "It looks like a regular deck of playing cards. But when you use the cards, the ink comes off and turns your hands completely black." He chuckled. "It's a lot of fun."

He held up a round clock. "This one makes a great gift," he said in his croaky voice. "It's called the Forever Alarm. Your friend sets it. Then when the alarm goes off in the morning, it can't be shut off. There's no way to turn it off. You can stomp on it or throw it against the wall or smash it with a hammer. It just keeps buzzing forever."

"Sweet," I said.

I saw something I might want to buy. But before I could examine it, Lexi shoved a little package in my face. "Sam, I think this is definitely for you," she said.

I gazed at the front: INSTA-GRO PETS.

"Check it out," Lexi said. "They are tiny sponge creatures that you drop into water. And then they grow into HUGE living pets!"

I read the side of the box: "'AMAZE your friends with a GIANT living, breathing creature!'"

Lexi laughed. "I think you just found the pet you've been dying for!"

"Tell you what," I said. "I'll buy it for *you*. I just found something cooler."

I grabbed the box off the shelf and showed it to her. It was called a Phoney-Phone. It looked just like a real cell phone. Only it was a candy dispenser.

You flip it open just like a phone. Squeeze the POWER button, and a little round candy pops out of the screen.

"Perfect for sneaking into school," I said. "I can eat candy all day, and no one will know."

Lexi studied the box. "You can't make calls on it?"

"No. It's not a phone. It's filled with candy," I said.

She turned to Jonathan Chiller. "Does the Insta-Gro Pet really work?"

He pushed his square glasses up on his nose and stared at her with his cold blue eyes. "Everything in my shop works," he said quietly. "You'll see. I think you'll have a lot of fun with these."

I handed him the two items. "I'll buy both things," I said.

His gold tooth flashed as he smiled. "Good choices," he said.

He carried them to the front counter. He wrapped the two items together in black wrapping paper. Then he carefully tied red ribbon around the package.

He pulled out a tiny doll — a purple-and-green Horror. It looked just like the big furry Horrors who were the park workers in HorrorLand.

"Take a little Horror home with you," Jonathan Chiller said. He attached it to the ribbon.

I reached into my jeans pocket for some money. But Chiller waved me away.

"Don't pay me now," he said. He narrowed his eyes behind the old-fashioned glasses. "You can pay me back *next time you see me*."

I took the package. I stared back at him.

NEXT time?

What did he mean by that?

PART TWO

I pressed the POWER button and popped a round orange candy into my mouth. "Want one? They're really sour." I raised the phone to Lexi.

She made a disgusted face and shoved my hand away. "You know sour candy makes me puke. One candy and I'll puke all over your shoes."

"Thanks for sharing that," I said. I popped another one into my mouth. Then I tucked the phone into the pocket of my T-shirt.

It was a warm, sunny Saturday afternoon. We'd been back home for a week. I met Lexi after her tennis lesson at City Courts, and we were walking toward my house.

She wore white tennis shorts and a silky gray vest over a white T-shirt. Her hair was still damp from her tennis game.

A blue-and-red neon sign over a little store caught my attention. It was glowing brightly even in the strong sunshine. LITTLE SHOP OF HAMSTERS.

"Is that a new pet store?" I asked.

I didn't wait for her answer. I tore across the street. Two teenagers on bikes swerved to miss me. They screamed some rude words and shook their fists at me.

I love pet stores. I eagerly peered through the glass door, but I couldn't see anything inside. I pushed the door open and stepped into the shop. Lexi hurried in right behind me.

The store was dark inside. The air felt hot and steamy. It smelled like a barn. Like straw and dirt and farm animals. A slowly spinning ceiling fan made the deep shadows dance in front of us.

"Whoa!" I let out a startled cry as I nearly bumped into a glass wall. I blinked and let my eyes adjust to the dim light.

An enormous display case filled the center of the shop. It had glass walls on all four sides and a glass top. A narrow sliding wire door was placed in one of the glass walls.

The case was taller than me. It had to be at least eight feet tall. And it was nearly as wide as the store.

From inside the walls of glass, eyes stared out at me. Dozens of tiny black eyes. The case was actually a cage! It had *hundreds* of hamsters packed inside.

Hamsters poked their noses against the glass, gazing out at Lexi and me. Behind them, hamsters scampered through the wood shavings that covered the cage floor.

What was that strange squeaking sound? Hamster wheels. There were eight or ten of them, with hamsters running hard, making them spin and squeal.

Hamsters were chomping away in the long row of food dishes on the back wall. Others ran through long, twisting plastic tubes. One big guy was trying to climb a side of the glass cage. Two hamsters were wrestling in a food dish.

"Lexi — it's like a big hamster circus!" I said.

She pressed her hands against the glass and peered in. "You mean like a hamster *city*!" she said. "The cage is bigger than my bedroom!"

"They are totally cute," I said. "Look how they wrinkle their noses."

She poked me. "Hey — check out the funny front teeth. That one looks just like you, Sam!"

"Ha-ha," I said, poking her back. "What a weird store. No dogs or birds or anything. Just hamsters. Hundreds of hamsters."

"Look. That one found a piece of carrot," Lexi said, pointing. "And the big brown one is waiting for him to drop it. Ready to pounce. This is a total riot!"

I watched a cute little gray hamster running on a wheel. The squeaking wheels were the only sounds in the shop, except for the hum of the ceiling fan.

"My parents won't let me get a dog," I told Lexi. "They say I have to prove I'm responsible first."

"Like I don't know that," Lexi said, staring into the cage. "Sam, you've told me that a thousand times!"

"But maybe they'll let me get a hamster," I said. "You don't have to walk a hamster or anything. It doesn't take much work."

Lexi started to answer. But her mouth dropped open and no sound came out. Her eyes bulged.

I turned and followed her gaze. And then I gasped as I squinted into the dim light and saw what she was staring at.

An *enormous* hamster — gigantic! — taller than Lexi and me — crept out from behind the cage. It walked on *two legs*, in a strange, shuffling motion.

Its glassy eyes — as big as tennis balls! — gazed straight ahead. Its huge front paws swung low at its bulging sides. Its fur ruffled by the wind from the ceiling fan.

It turned. It SAW us!

And its big paws thudded softly on the floor as it headed right for us!

7

"No!" A sharp cry escaped my throat.

The creature's huge eyes didn't blink. They stared hard at Lexi and me, glowing darkly.

The giant hamster moved in and out of the shadows cast down from the spinning ceiling fan. Lexi and I backed up against the glass cage. And watched it slowly advance, step by step.

And then it reached up with its big white front paws and lifted off its head.

Lexi and I burst out laughing.

A man in a hamster costume! He held the head in front of him. His face was red, and his forehead was dripping with sweat.

"Hot in this thing," he said.

His curly black-and-gray hair was drenched. He had dark eyes, a big round nose, and a bushy black mustache that looked like a paintbrush.

He set the hamster head down on the front counter. "Like my new store?" he asked. He pulled his arms free and climbed out of the costume.

"I'm Mr. Fitz." He was short and thin, but he had a deep voice. He put a white apron on and struggled to tie the straps. "Your names?"

We told him.

"Do you wear that costume all day long?" Lexi asked.

He picked up a towel and mopped his face and hair. "No," he said. "Just sometimes. It's an attention getter."

"Sure is," I said. "You really got *our* attention!" I decided not to tell him he nearly scared us to death!

"I wear it outside the shop to attract customers," Fitz said. "When you have a new store, you have to work hard to get people to notice you."

He shoved the costume under the counter.

"I like your store," I said. "It's totally cool."

"Sam is really into animals," Lexi said.

Fitz nodded. "Is that so?" He slid open the wire door to the glass cage. A few hamsters turned at the sound. The rest went on with what they were doing.

Fitz reached into the wood shavings and pulled up a hamster in each hand. Then he turned and handed one to Lexi and one to me.

My hamster was white with brown spots down his back. He squirmed in my hand. I almost dropped him. His pink nose twitched, and he gazed up at me with bright black eyes.

Lexi rubbed a finger down the back of her hamster. He was all white, except for a scattering of little brown spots on his face. They kind of looked like freckles.

"I love their fur," she said. "So soft." The hamster tried to nibble her finger. She turned it around in her hand.

"Totally awesome," I told Fitz.

He motioned to the little guy, who was trying to climb up my arm. "Do you want him, Sam? They're not very expensive."

"I wish," I said with a sigh. "I'd love a hamster. But my parents won't let me have a pet."

"He has to prove he's responsible first," Lexi chimed in.

Fitz eyed me. "You're not very responsible?"

"Yes, I am," I said. "It's just . . . they want me to prove I'd take good care of a pet."

Fitz nodded. "Well, you can come back here anytime and play with them."

The hamster tickled my hand with his nose. I handed him back to Fitz. "Thanks."

Lexi petted her hamster a little more, then she carried him to the cage and set him down. We started for the front door.

But Fitz stopped us. "Hey — want to help me give them water? I've got a lot of water bottles to fill."

He pulled two glass bottles from behind the counter.

"Sure," I said. I took one of them from him. "What's in this bottle? Just plain water?"

"It's called Vito-Vigor," Fitz answered. "It's vitamin water. You know. Like you buy at the supermarket."

He handed Lexi the other bottle of Vito-Vigor. Then he led us to the back of the cage. "Pour the water into these tubes," he said. "It runs into their water bottles."

I tilted the bottle and poured water into the tube that stuck out of the back of the cage. I could see it flow into the bottle on the other side of the glass.

"You have to go inside the cage to feed them and change the floor shavings," Fitz said.

"Look at them all staring up at us. They must think we're *giants* or something," Lexi said.

"Maybe they think we're *monsters*," I said. "Maybe they'll have nightmares about us."

Lexi laughed. "Sam, I *already* have nightmares about you!"

We filled all the water bottles, then handed Fitz the empty Vito-Vigor bottles.

"Well, thanks for your help, guys," he said. "Come back anytime."

We walked out and started toward my house.

Lexi had a strange smile on her face. She

had her arms wrapped tightly around the front of her vest.

We walked a few blocks, then she stopped. Her eyes flashed and her grin grew wider.

"Here, Sam," she said, "here's a present for you." She held out her hand.

And I let out a scream. "Lexi — are you CRAZY?"

8

Lexi dropped a hamster into my hands. She had hidden him under her vest.

"No way!" I cried. "No way!"

She grinned. "It's the freckly guy. I never put him back in the cage."

"But — but —" I sputtered.

Lexi shrugged. "What's the big deal, Sam? Fitz has hundreds of them. He won't miss one hamster!"

The hamster twitched his little nose at me. I could feel his little heart pounding.

I smoothed a finger down his back to calm him.

"Lexi, this is *stealing*!" I cried. "You *stole* this hamster!"

Her smile faded. She tugged her vest down. "I was only trying to help you," she said. "I know how desperate you are to have a pet."

"Not desperate enough to steal," I said. "Don't

help me, Lexi. That man Fitz is a nice guy. No way I'm going to steal a hamster from his store. That's just crazy."

Her cheeks turned red. "Okay. Fine. I'm crazy," she snapped. She balled her hands into tight fists. Then she spun away and stomped off.

"Hey, wait —" I called.

But she started to run. She tore down the block without looking back.

I raised the trembling hamster to my face and spoke gently to him. "Don't worry, fella. I'm going to take you back to your home."

I tucked the little guy into my shirt pocket to keep him safe. Then I hurried back to the hamster shop.

I peered into the front window. The store was pitch-black. Then I saw the little sign on the door: CLOSED.

I let out a groan. The hamster wriggled in my shirt pocket. I tucked my hand over him to make sure he didn't jump out.

I pounded on the door with my other fist. Maybe Mr. Fitz was somewhere in there.

My mind was spinning. Would he believe me when I told him what happened? Or would he think I stole the hamster?

But there was no sign of him.

I tried the door — and it swung open!

"Whoa!"

Now my heart was racing as fast as the hamster's! I stepped into the darkness and shut the door silently behind me.

It was hot and smelly in there. The ceiling fan was shut off. The back of my neck began to prickle. I felt a drop of sweat run down my forehead.

It was so dark, I could barely see into the glass cage. I could hear the hamster wheels squeaking. And I could hear their paws scratching the wood shavings as they scampered around.

I stepped closer to the glass. Hamsters stared out at me. They climbed over each other to get a better look.

I glanced all around. No sign of Fitz. The big hamster costume was crumpled on the counter. The head rested upside down.

The air felt steamy and thick. Hard to breathe.

I'll return the hamster to the cage and get OUT of here, I told myself.

I moved to the cage door. I reached into my pocket for the hamster — and POP!

The hamster stepped on the cell phone in my pocket. A sour candy flew out of the phone.

"Hey!" I let out a cry as the hamster grabbed the candy in his front paws. And stuffed it into his mouth. He swallowed the little candy without chewing.

I pulled the hamster from my pocket and raised him in front of me. "Are you okay, Freckle Face?" I asked him.

My chest felt fluttery. Had I just poisoned the little guy?

The hamster lowered his eyes to my pocket. He began to claw with both paws. He stretched his body, pawing for the pocket.

It made me laugh.

He was trying to get more candy!

I wrapped my hand tightly around the hamster and walked to the cage door. It took me a while to figure out how to open the sliding door. I slid the door open.

I tried to lower the hamster into the cage. But he grabbed the top of my T-shirt pocket with both paws — and wouldn't let go!

"Come on, dude. Get your paws off me!" I begged. "No more candy."

I wrapped both hands around the little guy's waist and tugged.

He lowered his head into my pocket and clung tightly to my shirt.

I heard rustling sounds. I looked down and saw hamsters darting toward the open cage door.

"No!" I cried.

I pictured a hundred hamsters escaping — scampering around the shop in the dark.

I moved to block the door. Stumbled — and staggered into the cage. I had to be so careful not to step on any of the hamsters!

Still gripping the hamster, I caught my balance on the cage floor. I reached behind me and slid the door shut before any hamsters could run out.

"Ohhhh." A powerful stench rolled over me. "It stinks in here!" I said out loud. My voice was muffled by the glass walls.

Doesn't Mr. Fitz ever clean out their poop?

I tried holding my breath. But I couldn't get the smell out of my nose.

I jumped as a creature ran over my foot. Too dark to see them. But I could feel hamsters brushing my legs. The wood shavings on the floor rustled as hamsters moved all around me.

I scolded myself. *What are you scared of, Sam? They're just cute little hamsters!*

But there were hundreds of them. I felt them run over my shoes and scratch at my legs. And all I could see were their eerie, glowing eyes. Eyes all around me.

"No more candy!" I told the hamster. I gave one more tug — and pulled him off my pocket.

I started to lower him to the cage floor — when the store lights flashed on.

Mr. Fitz stood outside the cage, his eyes blinking. When he saw me, they bulged wide in shock.

He scowled at me and let out an angry shout: "What are you DOING in there?"

I froze.

My brain locked.

How could I explain this?

Did he think I was a thief?

I still had the freckle-faced hamster wrapped tightly in my hand.

Mr. Fitz had his nose against the glass, studying me. He was definitely not happy to see me in there.

I set Freckle Face down on the cage floor. The hamster didn't scamper away to rejoin his friends. He just stood there on two legs, staring up at me.

Weird, I thought.

I turned and walked to the cage door. I could feel my shoes slide on sticky shavings on the floor. Holding my breath, I slid open the wire door. And stumbled out of the cage.

Fitz was watching me. He had his arms crossed in front of his white apron. "Sam, the store is closed," he said.

"I — I know," I stammered. "I . . . had to return a hamster."

He squinted at me. "Return it?"

I nodded. My mouth was suddenly very dry. "It got caught in Lexi's vest," I said. "She didn't see it till we got halfway to her house. The little guy was stuck to her. So . . . I . . . uh . . . brought him back."

Yes. I was lying. But I didn't want to get Lexi in trouble.

Did he believe me?

I couldn't tell. But the scowl faded from his face. "That was nice of you," he said finally. "Very responsible."

"I . . . knocked on the door," I said. "I guess you didn't hear me."

"No problem," Fitz said. "You just startled me."

He picked up a cloth and began wiping off the front of the cage. "These hamsters are real escape artists. They'll climb into your pants pocket if they think it will give them a few minutes of freedom!"

I laughed. "Well, they sure are cute," I said. "This little freckled one wouldn't let go of me."

"Well, thanks again," Fitz said. "Come back anytime, Sam. And tell your friends."

I let out a sigh of relief. I hoped he didn't hear it. I said good-bye. Then I hurried home to dinner — and more trouble!

Lexi came to dinner. She sat across from Noah and me. She didn't seem to be angry anymore. She didn't even mention hamsters.

Noah is three, and he's a real devil — only my parents think he's a riot. Take my word for it — he isn't a riot! Unless you spell riot *t-r-o-u-b-l-e*!

Noah looks a lot like me, except his hair is blond and wavy. He has the same dark eyes and the same bunny teeth as me. Maybe the worst thing about Noah? He likes to bite!

Dad sat in his usual chair at the end of the table. He's big and red-faced and tough. He was an NFL tackle for a year, before he hurt his knee. Now he manages a truck rental company.

He is always grumpy when he's hungry, so he didn't say much.

Mom is tiny and very pretty. She always sits at the other end, closest to the kitchen — and closest to Noah, in case he acts up. Which is *always*.

Tonight he started dinner by putting string beans up his nose. "Look what grows!" he called to Lexi. "Look what grows!"

He's always worse when Lexi is around. He likes to show off for her. Especially since she laughs at all his horrible jokes.

Lexi is way too nice to Noah. But she thinks he's adorable, just like my parents do.

I think he's adorable, too — if you spell adorable *h-o-r-r-i-b-l-e*!

We started passing around the chicken and potatoes. Noah spilled his apple juice onto his plate and started to laugh.

It was an accident. But why does he always think his accidents are so funny? Why doesn't he ever feel bad about them?

I grabbed my napkin and helped mop up the apple juice. "Be careful, Noah," Dad muttered. He didn't look up from his chicken legs.

Mom poured Noah another glass of juice.

Then things were calm for a while. After two or three chicken legs and a pile of mashed potatoes, Dad started to get in a better mood. Lexi talked about an e-mail she got from a girl she met at HorrorLand.

"Nice you made a new friend," Mom told her.

"I'm your friend," Noah said to Lexi. He had

mashed potatoes all over his cheeks — and in his EARS!

I decided to tell Mom and Dad about the new pet shop. I told them about the owner, Mr. Fitz, and how the store had one enormous glass case with hundreds of hamsters running around in it.

And then I said, "Can I have a hamster? Please please please?"

I didn't mean to beg. It just came out that way.

Dad shook his head no and kept chewing away on a chicken leg.

"You know the rule," Mom said. "You can have any pet you want as soon as you prove you're responsible."

"But how can I prove I'm responsible if I don't have a pet?" I demanded.

Mom scrunched up her face. She always does that when she's thinking hard. "Tell you what, Sam," she said. "I'll give you some tests. If you pass, we'll see about buying you a hamster."

I groaned. "What kind of tests?"

Noah raised himself to his knees on the chair next to me. "I'll be your pet," he said. He started panting like a dog. Then he began to lick my arm.

Mom, Dad, and Lexi burst out laughing.

Yuck. He was getting my arm sopping wet.

I tried to swing it free. But Noah grabbed on with both hands and kept licking. "Stop it!" I shouted. "Noah — give me a break! Down boy! Down!"

That made everyone laugh even harder.

"I'm your pet! I'm your pet!" Noah cried. And then he clawed my arm!

"*Ow!* Stop!" I shouted.

Lexi leaned across the table and whispered to me. "I can help you. I think I can distract him."

"Look! I'm a hamster!" Noah exclaimed. He bunched his hands into paws — and then he bit me!

11

Lexi reached into the pocket of her shorts and pulled out a little blue box. I recognized it. The Insta-Gro Pets from HorrorLand.

She struggled to open it. Finally, she ripped it open.

She pulled out a tiny piece of blue sponge. It was about the size of a quarter.

Noah dug his teeth into my skin.

"Please — hurry!" I cried.

Lexi plopped the little sponge creature into Noah's apple juice glass.

It fizzed for a few seconds. It began to crackle. Then it *POPPED*.

With a loud *WHOOOOSH*, the blue spongy stuff *exploded*! It blew up like a bubble-gum bubble.

CRAAAAACK. The juice glass shattered and flew apart. Apple juice went pouring over the table again.

The sponge creature inflated fast, rising like a

helium balloon. It bobbed from side to side, spreading itself over the table . . . growing wider, wider . . . taller.

Mom and Dad both screamed. Noah let go of my arm and dropped back into his chair.

The huge spongy creature thumped against Noah — and sent him toppling off his chair. The chair crashed to the floor.

"Monster!" Noah shouted. "Monster!"

The blue thing grew bigger . . . BIGGER. Its body was as big as a car! Its head tilted up like a *Tyrannosaurus rex*!

It jumped. Jumped again. Plates and food platters went sliding off the table. They clattered to the floor. Glasses shattered.

We all jumped to our feet. I stepped in broken glass as I stumbled back.

Mom had both hands pressed to her cheeks. She was screaming: "Do something! DO something!"

But the Insta-Gro Pet kept growing. It bobbed and bounced as it spread and grew.

THUD. THUD. THUD.

So heavy! I thought it might crack the dinner table!

Bawling at the top of his lungs, Noah backed into me.

Dad stood frozen, his face twisted in shock.

I raised my eyes as the creature's head banged the ceiling light. The fixture cracked, then came flying apart. Big pieces of glass shot down on us. The lightbulb shattered and went dark.

Noah kept yelling, "Monster! Monster!"

Lexi covered her head with her hands and screamed.

The creature's head jammed against the ceiling. The huge body tilted on the tabletop from side to side.

"It — it won't stop GROWING!" I cried. "LOOK OUT! It's going to FALL!"

It tilted over us. Bounced once. Twice. Then finally settled.

Silence.

A strange hush fell over the room. The only sound was Noah's sniffling sobs.

The enormous creature stood completely still. Its head poked up against the shattered ceiling light. Its huge body spread over the whole dining room table.

Mom crunched over the broken plates and glasses and hurried to hug Noah. "Are you okay?" she cried. "Is everyone okay?"

We all answered quietly. I think we were totally dazed.

"What a mess," Dad muttered. I looked down. Dad was standing on the chicken platter.

Mom hugged Noah. "What *is* that thing?" she cried.

"It — it's a toy we got at HorrorLand," I stammered.

Noah stuck a hand out and squeezed the blue Insta-Gro Pet body. It made a *scritchy* sound. Noah laughed. He grabbed it with both hands and squeezed.

"Noah — let go!" Mom pulled him away. "That thing is *dangerous*! And we don't know what it's *made* of!"

Noah laughed. "Me like it. Can me have one?"

Dad was scowling at me. He pointed to the big creature. "I'll bet this was Sam's idea."

"Well . . . yes," Lexi replied. "I mean, it's mine. But Sam got it for me."

"Lexi — please shut up!" I cried. "You're not helping!"

Dad shook his head. "Sam, you definitely flunked your first test."

"What test?" I cried in a high, shrill voice. "What do you mean? I didn't DO anything!"

A loud *POOOOF* made us all jump.

The giant creature tilted forward — so far, it almost crashed into the dining room window.

Then . . . *SCRITCH SCRITCH SCRITCH* . . . it began to shrink.

We all stood perfectly still and watched as it squeezed itself smaller and smaller. Like a balloon losing its air.

It took only a few seconds. And it was the size of a quarter again. It lay there in the center of the table — just a little blue dot surrounded by broken dishes. It didn't move.

Mom shook her head. "What a horrible thing!" she cried. "I've never seen anything so awful! At least it doesn't stay big for long. Now, everybody pitch in. Let's get this mess cleaned up."

Mom and Dad bent down and began picking up pieces of broken plates and broken glass. I hurried to the kitchen and brought the trash can to dump all the broken stuff.

Lexi came over to me and stuffed the package of Insta-Gro Pets into my hand. "*You* take this, Sam. It's too dangerous. I don't want it anymore."

"Hey — I don't want it, either," I told her. "No way." I tossed the package into the garbage can.

"Get the vacuum, Sam," Mom said. "Noah, be careful. There's broken glass everywhere. Go up to your room until we get it all vacuumed up."

"Me don't want to," Noah said. He crossed his skinny little arms in front of his chest and wouldn't move.

Cute kid, huh?

We vacuumed. We mopped. We swept. We did everything you can to clean up broken plates and glasses.

Dad kept glaring at me as we worked.

"It's not my fault! Really!" I cried. "Why do I get blamed for everything?"

"Who else would buy an Insta-Gro Pet?" Dad grumbled.

A short while later, Dad left to drive Lexi home. Mom was putting Noah to bed.

I trudged up to my room and plopped down at my desk. I picked up the cell phone candy dispenser and popped a sour candy into my mouth.

Yum.

I thought about that freckled hamster and how much he liked the candy. He was so eager to get more, he clung to my shirt pocket and wouldn't let go!

Well, they ARE good candies, I thought. *That hamster had good taste!*

I popped another one into my mouth.

"They're so tingly," I murmured. When it melted in my mouth, it made my whole face tingle.

No. My whole body. It made my whole body tingle.

Weird. What a weird feeling.

I popped another one into my mouth. I couldn't stop.

13

A few days later, Mom gave me my *real* first test.

She was standing at the mirror in the front hall, fiddling with a floppy maroon cap. She tucked her dark hair under the cap. Changed her mind. Let her hair fall back to her shoulders.

"I'm going out for a short while," she said.

"And you want me to watch Noah?" I asked.

She nodded, studying herself in the mirror. "Go up to his room and play with him," she said.

"No problem," I told her.

"Not too rough," Mom added.

"I hope you told Noah that!" I said. "He's always beating me up!"

Mom set the cap down and tossed back her hair. She started for the door. "Remember this is a test, Sam."

"I'll definitely pass!" I said. "I'm totally responsible, Mom. Really."

I followed her to the kitchen door. "I already

picked out a place for the hamster cage in my room," I said. "On the shelf near the window. So he will get a lot of sunlight. Know what I'm going to call my hamster?"

"Not now, Sam," Mom said. She opened the door to the garage.

"Hammy," I said. "That's a good name for a hamster, right? Hammy the Hamster?"

"Sam —"

"But I've been thinking. Maybe I need *two* hamsters. I mean, one hamster all by himself could get pretty lonely, don't you think?"

"Sam — please," Mom said. "Don't get ahead of yourself. You haven't passed the first test yet!" She stepped down into the garage. "Go play with Noah. Bye." The door closed behind her.

"Oh, right. Noah," I said.

Mom's car started up. I headed to Noah's room — but the front doorbell rang. I pulled open the door. "Oh, hi."

Lexi stood there wearing a black T-shirt with a bright yellow frowny face on the front and a short denim skirt over black tights. "I came to apologize," she said.

She pushed past me into the house. She had a yellow leaf caught in her hair. I pulled it out and handed it to her.

"I'm totally sorry," she said. "You know. About the other night. The Insta-Gro Pet and everything. Everyone blamed you. But it was my fault, too."

I shrugged. "That's old news," I said. "Noah was attacking me. You were only trying to help."

Lexi picked up my mom's maroon cap and tried it on. She turned it around a few times, tilted it this way and that, then put it down.

"What are you doing?" she asked.

"I'm watching Noah," I said.

"Oh, good. I can help." She searched in her bag and pulled out her iPhone. "You have to check this out, Sam. It's a new app I just got."

"What does it do?" I asked. I took the phone from her and squinted at the screen. "It looks like a bunch of chickens."

Lexi nodded. "Okay. Go ahead and tilt the phone. Watch."

I tilted the phone to its side. Two of the chickens laid eggs. "Cool," I said.

"It's a game," Lexi said. "You have to tilt it so all five chickens lay eggs."

I tilted it again. Nothing happened. Two chickens clucked, but no eggs.

"It's not as easy as it looks," Lexi said. "If you tilt it the wrong way, the eggs crack open, and you lose."

She took the phone from my hand. She held it up straight for a few seconds. Then she tilted it slowly.

Four chickens laid eggs.

"Almost!" Lexi cried. "Four out of five. See? It's not that easy."

"Let me try again," I said. "This is totally cool. The chickens are so real-looking."

I held the iPhone carefully. Tilted it slowly. One chicken flapped its wings loudly. Three chickens laid eggs.

Lexi laughed. "You're getting it. It takes practice."

I tried it a few more times. Then I let out a gasp.

"Noah!" I cried. "I forgot all about him!"

I raced up the stairs to my little brother's room. My heart was beating hard in my chest. How long had I been playing the chicken game? Five minutes? Ten?

I stopped in his doorway. I saw him down on the red carpet. And I screamed:

"NO! NOAH! NO! OH, NOOOOOO!"

14

My eyes practically bulged out of my head. I gaped at the little blue thing in Noah's chubby hand.

An Insta-Gro Pet!

Noah was down on the floor on his knees. He turned when I screamed and grinned at me. "Me grow big!" he said. "Sammy, me grow big!"

"NOOOO!" I let out another scream. I dove into the room. I dropped to the floor.

Too late. He stuffed the blue sponge creature into his mouth.

He started to chew.

My breath caught in my throat. I felt my heart skip a beat.

I grabbed Noah's head and chin. I struggled to pry his mouth open.

He twisted and squirmed. He fought me, clamping his jaws tight.

But with a burst of strength, I tugged open

his mouth. Poked two fingers between his teeth — and pulled out the blue Insta-Gro Pet!

"Gimme it!" Noah shouted. He swiped a hand at it. "Gimme it! Me grow big!"

I swung it out of his reach — and tossed it to Lexi at the door.

She dropped it. The little blue sponge creature rolled across the carpet.

I held Noah back. It wasn't easy. The little guy is stronger than he looks.

Lexi dove for the pet. She grabbed it off the carpet and stuffed it into the pocket of her denim skirt.

"Gimme it!" Noah wailed.

I saw the package with the rest of the Insta-Gro Pets on the floor near his bed. I plucked it off the carpet and jammed it safely into my jeans pocket.

I turned angrily to Noah, still on his knees on the floor. "You took this out of the garbage — didn't you!" I shouted. "Well, that's *bad*, Noah. Keep your paws out of the garbage — hear me?"

He opened his mouth in a loud wailing sob. His face turned nearly as red as the carpet. He tossed back his head and cried and cried. Little teardrops trickled down his red cheeks.

I turned to Lexi. "What's up with this? He's being a total baby."

"We need to distract him," Lexi replied. She had to shout over Noah's frantic screams.

"Quick! Show him the chicken game," I said.

She shook her head. "It's downstairs. I'll get it."

Noah sobbed and beat his fists on the carpet.

"Oh, wait," I said. "I know." I pulled the cell phone dispenser from my pocket. "Here, Noah — check it out. Want a candy?"

I popped an orange ball from the phone and slid it into Noah's mouth.

He started to suck on it. At least it made him stop crying.

He swallowed it and pointed to his mouth. "More. More candy."

Lexi laughed. "He's a tough guy," she said.

I popped another candy out of the phone. He grabbed it from me and jammed it between his lips.

"More! More candy!"

I started to squeeze the phone again. But a voice behind me at the bedroom door made me stop. I spun around. "Mom?"

She stomped into the room. "You're giving him *candy*?" she cried. "That's how you prove you're responsible, Sam? You stuff your little brother with *candy*?"

"More!" Noah demanded, holding out his hand. "More candy!"

I let out a long, sad sigh. "Can't I do *anything* right? I'll never get a pet now."

But suddenly, I had a great idea. I knew just how I would prove to Mom and Dad that I was *totally* responsible.

15

After school the next day, I hurried across town to the Little Shop of Hamsters.

The door swung open as I burst inside. I spotted Mr. Fitz behind the front counter. He was putting bottles of Vito-Vigor water onto the counter.

Hamster wheels squeaked inside the huge cage. Several hamsters were having a race, darting back and forth the length of the cage.

"Sam," Mr. Fitz said. "You're all out of breath."

I waited a few seconds for my heart to stop pounding. "I — I ran all the way from school," I said.

He ran his fingers through his curly black-gray hair and scratched his head. "Did you come here to buy a hamster?"

"No," I said. "I can't. Yet. Remember? I have to prove to my parents that I'm responsible."

"How's it going so far?" he asked.

He popped the top off a Vito-Vigor bottle. He stepped to the back of the cage and began to fill a water bottle.

I followed him. "Not great," I confessed. "There were a couple of bad things that happened. Not my fault."

He nodded.

"I had this idea," I said. "Maybe . . . well . . . maybe I could help out here in the store. You know. Do chores. Feed the hamsters, give them water or something."

Fitz's mustache twitched. He locked his dark eyes on me. "You mean an after-school job?"

I nodded. "You wouldn't have to pay me or anything," I said. "If I had a job here, I could prove I'm responsible with pets, right? My parents would be totally impressed."

Fitz's mustache twitched again. But his expression didn't change. "I don't know, Sam," he said. "This is a very small store."

"But I could help. I really could!" I insisted. "I'm very good with animals. Very careful. If you'd just give me a chance . . ."

Mr. Fitz hesitated a long while. "Well, why don't we give it a try?" he said finally. "I guess I could use the help. So many hamsters to take care of."

"Yes! Yes!" I cried, pumping my fists in the air.

He scratched his head again. "I could even pay you a little each week, Sam," he said.

"Thank you! Thank you!" I said.

A few hamsters peered out through the glass. They were probably wondering what was up out here.

"You can feed and water them," Fitz said. "And clean the cage. And do some other chores around the shop."

"That's awesome," I said.

"Tell you what," he added. "A couple of weeks from now, I'll phone your parents and tell them how responsible you've been." He smiled. "If it works out."

"Don't worry," I said. "I'll work really hard. And . . . and I'll study up on hamsters. I'll learn all about them so I can help you better. And —"

I didn't get to finish my sentence. The door jangled and swung open — and Lexi came bursting in.

"I *knew* I'd find you here, Sam," she said.

I couldn't wait to tell her my news. "Lexi, Mr. Fitz just gave me an after-school job!"

"Sweet," she said. She slid open the door to the hamster cage and lifted out a fat white-and-gray hamster. She cradled him in her hand and began to pet him gently.

"What's your job going to be?" Lexi asked me.

"I'm going to feed them," I said. "And do other chores around the shop."

"That's totally sweet," Lexi repeated. She turned to Mr. Fitz. "Can I have a job, too? I can help Sam or something."

I held my breath. *Why did Lexi always want to help me?*

Fitz shook his head. "I'm real sorry," he said. "But I don't think there's enough work in the shop for *three* people."

Lexi let out a sigh. She gently stroked the hamster in her hand. I could see how disappointed she was. She put him back in the cage.

Suddenly, her expression changed. She walked over to the counter and with her free hand picked up the head to the big hamster. "I could wear this," she told Fitz.

His eyes grew wide. "What do you mean?"

"I could wear the hamster costume outside. You know. Walk up and down the block in it. Get attention for the store."

"Okay," Fitz said. "Sounds like a plan. Sam will work *inside* the store, and you'll work *outside* in the costume."

"Excellent!" Lexi cried happily. She slapped Fitz a high five. He looked a little surprised by it.

"Tell you what," he said to her. "I'll pay you two dollars for every customer you bring into the shop."

Lexi slapped *me* a high five.

"I have to go downstairs and bring up a bag of wood shavings," Fitz said. "It comes in twenty-pound bags. Very heavy. You two watch the store while I'm down there."

He stepped around the giant glass cage and disappeared down the basement stairs at the back of the store.

"I am so totally *pumped*!" Lexi exclaimed. "This was such an *awesome* idea, Sam. We'll have so much fun here — and you'll prove to your parents how responsible you are."

I nodded. "Yes, and —"

I stopped with a gasp. A gasp of horror.

I uttered a weak cry. And then I grabbed Lexi's arm.

"Look!" I gasped. "Lexi — you left the cage door open. The hamsters — they're all ESCAPING!"

16

I slid the cage door shut. Then I dove to the floor and grabbed a hamster in each hand.

They squirmed like crazy. But I held on tight and pushed them back into the cage.

Lexi was racing around, pulling hamsters off the floor, tucking them under her arm. She had four or five of them safely captured. When she tried to push the hamsters into the cage, two escaped again.

Lexi let out a cry as they darted across the floor. She dove after them.

Hamsters were racing in all directions. I scooped up another one that was heading for the basement door.

I glanced up and saw two girls looking in the front window. "Don't let anyone open the front door!" I screamed at Lexi.

A hamster jumped over my shoes and ran behind the counter. I swung around. Grabbed another little guy off the floor. Jammed two more back into the cage.

Two more hamsters were heading toward the basement door. I took off after them — and then I stepped on something and heard a loud *SQUISSSSH*.

"Ohh, sick!" I moaned.

I tried to lift my foot. My shoe stuck to the floor.

My stomach lurched. I started to gag.

"Lexi — I — I just *squashed* one!" I stammered. "I think I'm going to be sick."

17

Lexi ran over. She had a hamster in each hand. She gazed down at my shoe.

And started to laugh.

"Sam, it's not a hamster," she said, shaking her head. "It's a sponge!"

"Huh?"

I reached down and pulled it off the bottom of my shoe. A sticky, dirty sponge. Mr. Fitz must have dropped it.

Lexi laughed so hard, she almost dropped the two hamsters.

"It's not funny!" I cried. "Hurry! I hear Fitz. He's coming up the stairs."

We tossed the last hamster back into the cage and slid the door closed — just as Fitz stepped back into the shop.

I was panting hard, gasping for breath. Lexi slumped against the wall of the hamster cage.

"Everything okay?" Fitz asked. He dropped a big green bag on the floor.

"Yeah. No problem," I said, still struggling to breathe. I gazed all around.

Were any escaped hamsters still running loose?

I wanted to strangle Lexi, just a little. I mean, it's nice to have a friend who always wants to hang with you. But why did she always have to turn everything into a total *disaster*?

"Can we start our jobs now, Mr. Fitz?" Lexi asked.

He scratched his mustache. "Well, why not? Good idea."

Lexi pulled the hamster costume off the counter. She lowered it to the floor and began to climb into it.

Fitz handed me the big green bag. "These are wood shavings, Sam. Climb into the cage and freshen up the floor. There's a shovel in the corner. Shovel out the old shavings and spread fresh ones."

"Shouldn't we remove the hamsters first?" I asked.

"No place to put them," Fitz answered. "Just work around them."

"No problem," I said. I tore open the bag. The shavings smelled like pine trees.

Fitz disappeared down the basement stairs again.

Lexi put on the hamster head. But after a few seconds, she pulled it off. She mopped her forehead with one furry paw.

"Wow. It's *hot* in this thing. Maybe you and I should trade jobs. You like to be outdoors, right?"

"No way," I said. "Don't complain. And don't mess up."

She placed a paw over her chest. "*Me* mess up? You're joking, right? I never mess up!"

"Listen, Lexi," I said, "everything has to go perfectly. Fitz says in a week or two, he'll call my parents and tell them how responsible I am. But if you mess up —"

"No problem," Lexi said. "I'm only here to help you, Sam."

I rolled my eyes and groaned.

She pulled the hamster head back on and walked out the front door.

I found the shovel and carried it into the hamster cage. The little guys scampered all around me as I stomped around inside the cage.

"Yuck." I almost gagged again. The stench inside was unbelievable!

My shoes slid over clumps of sticky stuff. It smelled sour. How could little hamsters poop this much? And it had to be at least two hundred degrees in here!

"Move out of the way, guys!" I said. "I've got to clean this place up. It stinks!"

I started to shovel up some of the old shavings. I knew the fresh wood shavings would help make it smell better.

I got down on my knees to spread the shavings over the floor. Shavings stuck to my jeans. Other stuff stuck to my jeans, too. Gross.

Next time, I'll wear a pair of old jeans, I decided.

Hamsters scampered over my legs. One tried to climb my arm. I gently placed him on the floor.

Through the glass, I could see Lexi outside. She was marching back and forth outside the store.

I dug into the bag and tossed a handful of shavings onto the floor. "Hey!" I cried out when I saw a hamster standing on its hind legs, perfectly still. The hamster stared hard at me.

I lowered my head to stare back at it. And I saw the tiny freckles above his nose.

Yes, it was definitely Freckle Face. The same hamster. The one Lexi stole!

Without warning, he leaped at me. He grabbed on to my shirt pocket with both front paws.

"Whoa! How did you *do* that?" I cried. "Are you SUPER-Hamster?"

I tried to shake him off me. But he clung tightly and pulled himself up to my pocket.

"Let go! Hey! What do you think you're doing?" I shouted. "Come on, hamster — let *go* of me!"

18

The cell phone candy dispenser fell from my pocket and landed on the floor. The hamster let go of my shirt and dove after it.

I laughed. I finally realized what the little dude wanted.

"More candy?" I asked it. "You want another candy?"

I grabbed the dispenser. "It must be tastier than seeds," I said. "Okay, fella. I'll give you one. But just *one!*"

I popped a candy into the air — and *another hamster* grabbed it!

The second hamster shoved the candy into his mouth and gulped it down.

Freckle Face didn't move. He stared up at the candy dispenser.

I laughed again. "Your pal stole your candy!"

Both hamsters had their eyes on the phone in my hand. I lowered it toward the first little guy and squeezed out two more candies.

71

The candy balls dropped to the floor and disappeared under the wood shavings.

They both began to dig frantically, tossing shavings aside, burrowing with their noses.

"Oh, wow!"

They each grabbed a candy and shoved it into their mouths.

And then, as I watched in shock, they turned and *attacked* each other!

"Hey — stop!" I couldn't believe my eyes.

The two hamsters began to claw at each other, nipping furiously at each other's throats!

They clamped their paws around each other — and began wrestling around in the shavings and the muck on the floor.

Biting, kicking. Growling! A wild, desperate battle.

This is IMPOSSIBLE!

I knew instantly what had happened. The candy. One little piece of the orange candy had turned them wild. Made them crazy and wired.

Cute little hamsters turned into fierce fighters!

What a horrible mistake. But how could I know the candy would do this to them?

Freckle Face let out a whimper as the other hamster clawed furiously at his belly.

"Hey, Sam — how's it going in there?" I heard Fitz call to me through the glass.

"Uh . . . fine!" I shouted back. "No problem!"

I couldn't let him know. I couldn't let him see what I had done to his hamsters.

I crawled forward to block Fitz's view of the hamster fight. Then I grabbed a hamster in each hand and pulled them apart.

"Hey!" I let out a startled cry as they wriggled free.

Freckle Face leaped to my shoulder and began to claw furiously at my neck.

The other hamster sank his teeth into my wrist.

"Owww!" I couldn't hold back my scream.

Did Mr. Fitz hear me?

Freckle Face dove to my arm and clawed a hole in my shirt. The other hamster bit the back of my hand.

I twisted in pain. I felt a trickle of warm blood on my wrist.

I swung my hand hard — and sent the vicious little creature flying across the cage.

Then I grabbed Freckle Face around the middle and tugged him off my arm.

My heart pounding, I grabbed the shovel and started crawling to the cage door. But before I reached it, the two snarling hamsters came running at me on all fours.

They jumped onto the backs of my legs, scratching and biting.

I twisted around and smacked them off with my hand.

I gasped when I saw the froth pouring over their chins. Their eyes bulged crazily. They were snarling like angry dogs!

Before they could attack again, I slid open the cage door and staggered out.

I shoved the door shut behind me.

I grabbed my knees and struggled to catch my breath.

"What have I done?" I muttered. "What have I done to those hamsters?"

19

I frantically tried to brush myself off. But my jeans were totally covered in wood shavings and sticky hamster poop. My T-shirt sleeve was ripped. My shoes were covered in gunk.

"Mr. Fitz?" I called, my voice hoarse and trembling.

"He went back downstairs." I turned and saw Lexi leaning on the front counter.

The hamster head lay on the counter next to her. She had a bottle of Vito-Vigor tilted to her mouth, and she was gulping down the whole bottle without taking a breath.

She finished the drink, then wiped her mouth with a furry costume paw. "It's *boiling* in this costume!" she cried. "I need air-conditioning or something inside here!"

She set the empty bottle down behind the counter. Then she squinted at me. "Yuck. What happened to *you*?"

I shook my head. "I got dirty cleaning the cage," I said. I didn't want to tell her the truth. I wasn't sure she'd believe me about the hamsters turning vicious!

"Sam, you're a total mess," Lexi said.

"Tell me about it," I groaned. I decided to change the subject. "Did you bring in any customers?"

She sighed. "No. Some drivers honked at me. But nobody stopped. Some kids came walking by. But they said they didn't want hamsters because they're just rats without tails."

Fitz stepped out from the basement doorway. He gazed into the cage and smiled. "Good job with the shavings, Sam," he said.

"Uh . . . thanks." Didn't he see I was covered in scratches?

He checked his watch. "It's getting late," he said. "See you two after school tomorrow?"

"Excellent!" Lexi said.

I just wanted to get out of there and clear my head. I knew I had messed up.

It will all go back to normal tomorrow, I told myself.

I started out the front door — but turned back for a final glance at the cage.

The two hamsters were standing on their hind legs, noses pressed to the glass. Watching me.

Watching . . .

20

After dinner, I played with Noah for a while. He pretended to be a hamster, and I had to chase after him all over the upstairs. Then he pulled me down to the floor. He jumped on me and tried to lick my neck.

When I pushed him away, it made him angry. I grabbed him under his arms and raised him into the air.

That made him even angrier. He started kicking his feet, struggling to push himself down onto me.

He's pretty strong. But I held him up there till he turned red in the face.

Finally, he said, "No more hamster game. Me quit!"

I lowered him to the floor. His hands were squeezed into little fists. His face was still red. "No more hamster!" he shouted.

Dad appeared in the hall. "Sam, what were you doing to Noah?" he asked.

"We were just playing," I said.

"No more hamster! No more hamster!" Noah pounded his fists on the wall.

"Why did you get him all crazy and wired before bedtime?" Dad demanded.

I shrugged. "He's always crazy and wired."

Mom came to put Noah to bed.

"Me wired," he told her. "Me very wired."

That made them both laugh their heads off. I told you — they think Noah is a riot.

Dad followed me into my room. I sighed. "I have so much homework, I'll be up all night."

I dropped down in front of my computer. Dad squeezed my shoulders. "How's the job going?" he asked.

"Good," I said. I *had* to lie — right?

"What are you doing in the shop, Sam?"

"Just helping out. You know. Feeding the hamsters and stuff."

"And Mr. Fitz is a nice guy?" Dad asked.

I nodded. "Yeah. He's nice to Lexi and me. It's pretty quiet there. He doesn't have many customers."

"Maybe he should sell dogs and cats and birds and other animals," Dad said.

"Maybe," I said. "Or maybe hamsters will become a total craze. You know. And everyone will want one. And Mr. Fitz will become the richest pet store owner in America!"

Dad laughed. "Maybe," he said. "Well . . . Mom

and I are proud of you, Sam. If you keep this job and Mr. Fitz gives you a good report, we'll get you any pet you want."

"Really?" I turned to my dad with a big grin on my face. "Can I have an elephant?"

Dad laughed. "Do you really want to clean up after an elephant?"

"Probably not," I said. "But don't worry, Dad. You'll get a good report from Mr. Fitz. I promise."

Dad went downstairs. I was feeling pretty good. *Any pet I want . . .*

Sweet.

I just needed a good report from Mr. Fitz.

Uh-oh. How was I going to get that?

My good feeling lasted only a few seconds. A wave of dread fell over me. I let out a long sigh.

I pictured the two hamsters, crazed, clawing each other, wrestling furiously on the cage floor.

Snarling and growling and biting. Cute, cuddly hamsters — and they had ATTACKED me!

The candy turned them mean.

But how?

I'd been gulping it down ever since I got home from HorrorLand. I'd eaten *tons* of the little round candies. And I was exactly the same. The candy hadn't changed me. It made my face tingle a little. But it hadn't turned me mean.

I reached into my shirt pocket for the candy dispenser.

Uh-oh. Not there.

I searched my jeans pockets.

And then I gasped and let out a moan. "Oh, nooooo."

I must have left the candy in the hamster cage!

21

The next morning in class, what do you think I was thinking about?

Well, I definitely wasn't thinking about Civil War battles. My teacher, Mr. Pilcher, started a slide show about them.

But I had a different slide show going in my head. It was about hamsters!

Ferocious hamsters, growling and baring their teeth. Biting and clawing, frothing at the mouth, scratching each other's eyes out.

The pictures in my brain were totally disturbing. They kept me up all night. And now the next morning, I *wanted* to concentrate on Civil War battles. I really did.

But all I could think of was getting back into that cage and grabbing my candy dispenser before it could do any more harm.

After school, I jumped on my bike and began to pedal furiously.

But before I even reached the street, I heard Lexi shouting to me. "Wait up! Sam — wait up!"

I turned and let out a startled cry. "Lexi? What's up with *that*?"

She came stumbling across the grass in her hamster costume. She had the head tucked under her arm. "Give me a break, Sam! Can't you wait up?"

"Why are you wearing that? Did you run out of school clothes?"

She rolled her eyes. "Ha-ha. I just brought it to my drama class to show it off. Everyone thought it was totally cool."

I groaned. "I'm kind of in a hurry," I said.

"I'll jog beside you," Lexi replied. "Here." She shoved the hamster head over my handlebars.

"How are you going to jog in that costume?" I asked.

She shrugged. "I'll do my best. What's your big hurry, anyway?"

As we made our way slowly down the street, I explained to her why I was in such a hurry.

"Don't you see?" I said. "That candy is dangerous. I've got to get it out of that cage before more hamsters go crazy."

She stumbled. Grabbed on to my handlebars to keep herself from falling. And nearly pulled my bike over.

"I get it," she said. "You want to get into the cage and grab your candy phone back before Fitz sees that you left it there."

"Right," I said. I squeezed on the brakes as a squirrel ran across the street inches in front of us.

"I can help you," Lexi said.

I groaned. "Oh, please," I begged. "*Please* don't help me."

"No. Really," she said. She rubbed the thick fur on her chest with both paws. "I'll get Fitz's attention. I'll keep him busy while you climb into the cage."

"Well . . . okay," I said. "Sounds like a plan."

She was hobbling in the dumb costume. At this rate, it would take half an hour to get to the shop.

"Sam, if you've turned those cute little creatures into vicious beasts, you'll be in major trouble."

"Oh, thanks for sharing that," I said. "That cheers me up a lot! And by the way," I said, "you look ridiculous walking down the street in that costume."

"Just doing my job," Lexi said.

A few minutes later, I locked my bike in front of the shop. Lexi grabbed the hamster head and tugged it down over her head. Then she led the way inside.

Fitz was sitting on a tall stool behind the front counter, reading a magazine. But I was too worried to stop and talk to him. I rushed up to the big cage and peered in through the glass.

Had the hamsters turned into vicious beasts?

No. They were burrowing in the shavings, darting back and forth . . . running on their wheels.

Totally normal?

Maybe.

I *had* to get into that cage and find that candy phone.

I turned and saw Lexi talking to Mr. Fitz. She was tugging at the hamster head.

"I . . . I can't get it off," she told him. "It's stuck!"

She pretended to pull on the big mask.

Good work, Lexi! I thought. *Keep Fitz busy over there.*

Fitz turned his back to me. He began tugging at Lexi's costume. She pretended to tug at it, too. But I knew she was holding the head on.

Silently, I made my way to the cage door. I reached for it — and then froze.

A chill ran down the back of my neck.

I remembered the bites. The deep scratches.

Hamsters are tiny, furry little adorable creatures, right?

Was I really *terrified* of them now?

Did I have good reason to be?

I took a deep breath. Raised a trembling hand. Slid open the cage door — and carefully stepped inside.

22

The sharp pine aroma greeted me. My shoes scraped over the shavings.

Hamsters scampered over my feet. Three or four of them were running in circles, chasing each other. I looked for Freckle Face and his fierce pal. But I didn't see them.

I peered out into the shop. Fitz had his back to me. He and Lexi were still wrestling with the hamster costume.

I dropped to my hands and knees. I kept a lookout for the two vicious hamsters. I ran my hands through the thick carpet of wood shavings.

Where was the phone? Where did I drop it?

Maybe near the back wall of the cage, with all the food dishes and water. I crawled to that side and began to search.

Carefully, I slid my hands along the cage bottom. I pushed shavings out of the way and kept my eyes low, glancing back and forth.

I moved slowly from one end of the cage to the other. Then I started back again.

No sign of it. Why couldn't I find it?

Where was it? *Where?*

The air grew stifling hot inside the cage. I could just barely hear Fitz and Lexi talking over the squeal of the whirling hamster wheels.

My heart was pounding hard, and I was drenched in sweat. I began to search more frantically. I tossed shavings out of my way. I crawled slowly from one end of the cage to the other.

No sign of the candy dispenser.

Suddenly, I stopped with a gasp. What was that sound?

Was that a *growl*? A hamster growl?

Take it easy, Sam, I scolded myself. *Don't lose it now.*

I peered out through the glass. I saw Fitz pull Lexi's hamster head off.

Lexi's face was bright red. She took a bottle of Vito-Vigor, raised it to her mouth, and began to drink it down.

Fitz had his back to her. He was staring at the cage. His eyes went wide when he saw me on my hands and knees inside it.

He slid open the door and leaned in. "Sam? What on earth are you doing in there?"

I had to think fast. "Uh . . . just cleaning up a bit," I said.

"Good," Fitz said. "I like it that you go right to work and don't have to be told. Very responsible, Sam."

"Thanks," I said. "I want to do a good job."

My eyes were still searching for that candy phone.

"Be sure to fill all the water bowls and food dishes," Fitz said. "I have to go out for a while."

"No problem," I said.

I watched him say good-bye to Lexi. Then he pulled on a jacket and hurried out the front door.

As soon as he was gone, Lexi hurried to the side of the cage. "Did you find it?" she shouted.

I shook my head. "Not yet. It's got to be here somewhere."

"Keep looking," she said. She slid the hamster head down over her face. Then she turned and hurried outside to do her job.

I moved up and down the cage, searching desperately. Sweat poured down my forehead. My arms and legs ached from being down on the cage floor for so long.

"Where is it? Where is it?" I started to mutter to myself.

Two or three hamsters turned to stare at me. Did they think I was talking to *them*?

I heard another growl. *Hamsters* growling! I could hardly believe it.

I bent down to scoop away wood shavings. A

hamster leaped onto my back. Then he instantly jumped back to the cage floor.

I heard another soft growl. Almost like a *warning*.

I have to get out of here, I thought.

And then my hand bumped something hard. I wrapped my fingers around it and pulled it up.

The candy dispenser. I found it!

I let out a victory cry. "YAAAAAAY!"

I was happy — but not for long.

I held the phone close to my face and shook it. It was EMPTY.

23

I sat up. I shook the phone again.

No. No candy.

"I don't believe it!" I cried.

I jammed the phone into my jeans pocket. Did they eat it all?

I looked down. A bunch of hamsters had lined up in front of me. They sat on their haunches, very still, staring up at me. Their round black eyes glowed.

They sniffed the air.

"Boo!" I waved both arms and shouted at the top of my lungs. I figured that would scatter them.

But they didn't move.

There were at least ten of them. One made a snarling sound and bared his teeth.

Another one uttered a low growl.

This isn't happening, I told myself.

Three or four more hamsters joined them. I realized they were forming a circle around me.

Two hamsters growled. The sound came from deep in their chests. A tiny brown-and-white hamster snapped his jaws.

"Give me a break, guys," I said. "Pick on someone your own size."

I meant it as a joke. But my voice trembled.

My chest felt all fluttery. My sweat suddenly felt cold on my forehead.

Something very weird was happening here. Something totally strange and frightening. *And it was all MY fault!*

It had to be the candy. It changed them. It changed their personalities.

It definitely turned them mean.

I stared down at the circle of growling hamsters.

How many of them had eaten the candy?

Had I ruined Fitz's hamsters *forever*?

If he knew I poisoned his hamsters by leaving the stupid candy in their cage, he'd . . . he'd kick me out of the shop. Fire me.

My parents would find out. And I'd be *fifty* years old before I ever got a pet!

I looked down. Hamsters bared their teeth and snapped their jaws. Several raised up on their hind legs.

Fear sent a chill down my body. They were seriously starting to creep me out.

I recognized Freckle Face. He stared up at me coldly. He clawed the air with both paws.

"Sam? What are you doing?"

The voice startled me. I gasped and stumbled back against the cage wall.

I blinked. Spun around. And saw Fitz poking his head through the half-open cage door.

"I've been calling to you. Is everything okay?" he asked.

"Uh . . . yeah," I said. "Fine."

"Glad you're having fun in there," he said. "But you haven't done your chores. Did you forget about the water and the fresh food?"

"No. I didn't forget," I said. "I was just . . . uh . . . playing with them a little."

A few hamsters growled. Did Fitz hear them?

He stared into the cage. His eyes narrowed as if he was thinking about something.

A hamster snapped his teeth at my ankle.

I swept him off and stumbled to the cage door. I stepped out quickly and slid the door shut. The hamsters still stood in a circle on their hind legs, staring out at me.

A feeling of dread tightened my throat.

I stared at the growling hamsters. They clawed the air and snapped their jaws.

It sounds crazy, I know. They were just little hamsters.

But my whole body shuddered with fear.

I really didn't want to go back in that cage.

They were waiting for me. I knew it.

After dinner, I hurried to my room. I opened my history book, but I couldn't read a word. My mind was spinning.

My phone rang. It was Lexi. "Sam, what happened?" she asked. "Why did you run out of the shop without doing your work? Are you okay?"

"I . . . I told Fitz I felt sick," I said. "And I really did. Something terrible has happened."

"Oh, wow," Lexi muttered. "The candy?"

"Yes. The candy." I groaned. "They ate it all. The phone was totally empty."

"How much candy was in the dispenser?"

"A lot!" I said.

"And you really think it turned them mean?" Lexi asked.

"I don't *think* it. I *know* it. They were growling and baring their teeth and snapping their jaws. They surrounded me, Lexi. They were getting ready to chew me to pieces!"

"I don't believe this," Lexi murmured into the phone. "Tiny hamsters?"

"You've got to believe me," I said. "I know they're tiny. But they're terrifying. They were going to gang up on me and —"

"Okay, okay," she said. "Maybe I can help you."

Oh, noooo, I thought. *Whenever Lexi tries to help me, it's a disaster!*

"I'm desperate," I said. "How can you help me?"

"Well . . . I have an idea," she replied. "Did you save the box the cell phone came in?"

"The box?" I thought hard. "Maybe. I don't remember."

"If you have the box," Lexi said, "you can find the e-mail address or the phone number of the candy company. And you can contact them and ask them what to do."

"Huh?" My mind started to spin. "How can I ask them what to do?"

"Easy," Lexi said. "Ask them if anyone else ever complained about their candy turning pets or anyone mean. Ask if they know something you can give them to change them back to normal."

"That sounds a little crazy," I said.

"Worth a try, Sam. Really. It's worth a try."

"But, Lexi —"

I heard a loud clicking on the phone.

"I've got another call," Lexi said. "Got to go. Bye."

"But wait —"

She clicked off. I stared at the phone in my hand. Maybe for once Lexi had actually come up with a helpful idea.

But did I keep the box?

I searched the bottom of my clothes closet where I always toss stuff. I found the little stuffed Horror that gift-shop guy had given me. It was leaning against the back wall next to a box of old CD's.

Down on my hands and knees, I kept searching. And there was the box under a pile of dirty T-shirts. PHONEY-PHONE.

It had a picture of the phone on the front with a bunch of little red and blue candies popping out of the screen. Behind the phone, you could see a boy's face. His eyes were bulging out of his head, and he had a big grin from ear to ear.

I turned the box over and read the tiny type on the back. Yes. I found the company name: *Phoney-Phone Productions*. And in even tinier type, a phone number.

"Will they know how to help me get the hamsters back to normal?" I asked myself out loud.

I punched in their number. After two rings, a recorded woman's voice came on:

"Thank you for calling Phoney-Phone. If you

would like to buy a new phone, press one. If you would like to order some candy refills, press two. If you are having a problem with your phone . . ."

I didn't wait for her to finish. I pressed three.

Some jingly music came on. Like you hear in supermarkets. I sat down on the edge of my bed and waited with the phone pressed to my ear.

After three or four minutes, a man spoke: "This is Mr. Dover. How can I help you?"

"Uh . . . Mr. Dover," I started. "I'm having a little trouble with my candy dispenser phone."

"Is it jammed?" he asked. "When you shake it, can you hear candy rolling inside it?"

"Well . . . my problem is a little different," I said. "You see, I work in a hamster store."

"Excuse me? A hamster store?" he interrupted. "You mean a store that sells only hamsters?"

"Yes," I said. "And the hamsters ate the candy. And it turned them mean. I mean, totally fierce."

"You called to tell me that our candy turned a bunch of hamsters mean?" he asked.

"Yes. And I wondered if you know something I can give them to turn them back to normal."

There was a long silence on the other end. Then Mr. Dover said: "What color candy was it?"

"Orange," I said.

I heard him gasp. "Hamsters ate the *orange* candy?"

"Yes," I replied. I suddenly had a heavy feeling in the pit of my stomach.

Another long silence. Then he asked in a quiet voice, "Young man, *you* didn't eat the orange candy — did you?"

"Well, yes," I told him. "I ate a lot of it."

"Oh, wow," Mr. Dover said. "Oh, wow."

"Wh-what's wrong?" I stammered.

"The orange candy wasn't supposed to be sold," he said. "We recalled all the orange candy. We took it back. There was a mistake at the factory, see? The wrong ingredient accidentally went into the orange ones."

I swallowed. My mouth suddenly felt very dry. "The wrong ingredient?"

"Yes, it's a flesh-eating chemical. First it turns you mean. Then it eats all your organs. It eats up your entire insides. Then it eats your eyeballs. In less than a week, there's nothing left but skin and bones."

25

It was my turn to be silent.

I pictured myself popping candy after candy into my mouth. And then I remembered feeding them to Noah.

I pictured all the little hamsters. I tried to imagine what it would feel like to have something eating up your insides.

The thought made my whole body shudder.

And then I heard loud laughter in my ear.

It took me a few seconds to realize it was Mr. Dover, laughing his head off.

"That was good!" he exclaimed when he finally stopped laughing. "Good story, kid. Hamsters turning mean because of our candy. I love it. Really."

"You — you were *joking*? You don't believe me?" I asked in a shaky voice.

"Are you having a party with a bunch of your friends?" Dover asked. "Making funny phone calls, right? You're going to put this on the Internet?"

"No. No way," I said. "I —"

He laughed again. He had a loud donkey laugh. Sort of "hee-haw hee-haw."

"I got you back," he said finally. "I think maybe you believed that flesh-eating stuff. You're not the only joker in the world, kid."

I took a deep breath. "Please listen," I begged. "I'm not a joker. The candy —"

"Can I send you a free candy refill?" Dover asked. "You gave me the best laugh of the day. An all-hamster store. Love it. Love it! You've got a great imagination, dude."

"But — but —"

"Give me your name and address. I'll send you a free refill."

"No thanks," I said.

I hung up.

Well, THAT went well! I thought.

I sat on the edge of my bed, rolling the Phoney-Phone box between my hands. I rolled it faster and faster. Then I crushed the box with both hands. Crushed it and tossed it against the wall.

Now what?

Was I really responsible for turning those fuzzy, cuddly little animals into vicious beasts?

26

After school, I made my way to the Little Shop of Hamsters.

I didn't exactly hurry. It's impossible to walk fast when your stomach feels as if it has a bowling ball inside it. And your legs are as shaky as jelly.

I walked with my head down, hands stuffed in my jeans pockets. I kept going over and over how I would tell Mr. Fitz what had happened.

I stopped in front of the shop. Clouds rolled over the sun, sending a blanket of shadow over the store. The sky turned dark — dark as my mood.

I took a deep breath. I tried to fight back the fluttery feeling in my chest.

Then I pushed open the door and stepped inside.

Fitz sat on a tall stool behind the counter. He was reading a paperback book. He looked up as I walked in.

"Mr. Fitz, I have to tell you something," I said. My voice came out shaky and high. My tongue felt dry and as big as a hamster!

I lowered my eyes. I stared at the floor. I couldn't bear to look at him.

"Something bad happened," I said. "I had this candy dispenser, which I accidentally left in the hamster cage. Before I could get it back, the hamsters ate all the candy."

I kept my eyes down, avoiding his stare. "And the candy changed them, Mr. Fitz. I know it's hard to believe about cute little hamsters. But the candy turned them mean. They growl and snarl now. And they bite and scratch. Really."

I shut my eyes. "Maybe you already noticed. Maybe you already saw the difference. I . . . I'm so, so sorry," I stammered. "Really. It was all an accident. But I had to tell you. I think they're ruined! I think I turned them into *monsters* or something!"

Eyes shut, I waited for him to say something.

Finally, he broke the silence. "Get in the cage, Sam," he said. "Go ahead. Get in the cage."

27

"Huh?" I let out a gasp. I opened my eyes.

And I saw the white earbuds in Mr. Fitz's ears. He pulled them out, and I could hear loud, tinny music pouring out of them.

I hadn't really looked at him. I hadn't seen that he had an iPod on the whole time.

"Mr. Fitz?" I asked. "You didn't hear a word I said — *did* you?"

He rubbed the front of his apron. "No. Sorry. Better get in the cage and freshen up the wood shavings, Sam," he said. "The hamsters are acting a little strange. I think it's because the cage wasn't cleaned yesterday. With so many hamsters, we have to clean it all the time."

"You don't understand —" I started.

Fitz dragged a big green bag across the floor. "Here are the fresh shavings," he said. He dumped the bag into my arms. "Go to work, fella."

I had no choice.

I glanced into the cage. I saw several of the little creatures watching me. They had their noses pressed up against the glass.

Their eyes were wild. A few of them were gnashing their teeth. One clawed at the glass frantically with both front paws.

My hand shook. I started to slide the cage door open. My heart was pounding like a drum machine.

Am I heading to my DOOM?

I put a shovel, a bucket, and the big bag of shavings into the cage. I slid the door open all the way. I took a deep breath and stepped in.

At least a dozen hamsters turned to watch me. More of them came darting forward to join the others.

I dropped to my knees and began to scoop old shavings into the bucket.

The hamsters bunched close together. Their fur bristled. Their noses twitched furiously. They all began to growl menacingly.

"Please — stop." The words escaped my throat.

Hamsters snarled and raked the air with their paws. Several tilted their heads back and uttered roaring growls.

"Give me a break!" I cried. "Please —"

They jammed forward. Like an angry mob.

Their black eyes were wide, all trained on me. They snapped their teeth.

On my knees, I turned and peered out through the glass. Was Fitz watching this?

No. I saw him heading to the basement.

"All alone," I muttered.

Hamsters lowered their heads, as if preparing to attack. Their low growls rang off the glass cage walls.

Their fur stuck straight up on their backs. Down on all fours, their bodies tensed.

And then I heard their paws scrape the cage floor. The wood shavings flew in all directions as the roaring hamsters attacked.

28

I let out a cry and tried to scramble to my feet. But I stumbled and toppled onto my back.

The snarling hamsters thudded closer, kicking up the wood shavings.

I pulled myself to a sitting position — and tensed my whole body, preparing for their attack.

But to my shock, they turned — and attacked EACH OTHER!

As I gaped in horror, the furious hamsters wrestled, rolling over and over. They clawed at each other's eyes. They scratched and bit and punched.

"This . . . can't be happening!" I murmured.

Shrill wails of pain rose up over the snarls and fierce growls.

A hamster lay on his back, kicking another hamster with all four paws. The other hamster dug his teeth into his opponent's belly. Shrieking, the two rolled over each other.

"STOP it! STOP it!" I screamed.

I pulled myself onto my knees.

The whole cage rang with wails and cries and furious growls.

Hamsters flew at each other, biting and clawing. Hamster fur floated in the air like blowing snow.

My first thought was to get OUT of there! Escape from the cage as fast as I could.

But I knew I had to stop this.

If Fitz saw this, I'd be dead meat. He'd have to close his store. And it would be all my fault!

Would he sue my dad?

I couldn't run away. I had to break up this horrible battle. But how?

I lurched forward and grabbed two wrestling hamsters. I pulled them apart. They clawed the air, squirming and twisting in my hands.

I separated them. Set them down on opposite sides of the cage.

Then I tugged two more battling creatures apart. I lifted them high. They screeched and clawed.

"OWWW!" I uttered a cry as one of them dug his teeth into my wrist.

The hamster slipped from my hand.

I shook my arm. I saw a few drops of bright red blood on the back of my hand.

In front of me, four snarling hamsters were in a raging battle. They were head-butting each other, ramming each other hard. They uttered squeals of pain. But it didn't stop their furious fight.

I pulled one up off the cage floor. He clawed my hand.

I felt a sharp pain at my ankle. *"OWWW!"* I spun around to see a hamster with his teeth dug into my leg.

Another hamster leaped onto my shirtsleeve. A hamster climbed my leg and clung to my jeans pocket.

Did he think the candy dispenser was in there?

"OWWW!" I felt another bite on my leg.

A hamster leaped onto the back of my neck. I felt him scratching at my head.

I grabbed him with both hands and lowered him to the cage floor.

"I'm not going to win this fight," I murmured. "No way I can break this up."

There were too many of them. And they were too vicious.

I had no choice. I had to get out of there. These hamsters could claw me to shreds!

I tugged two more hamsters off my sleeve. I shook one off my knee.

Then I spun around. I dove to the cage door. I grabbed the handle and pulled.

It didn't slide.

"Hey!" I uttered a shocked cry.

Two hamsters were climbing up my jeans.
I shook them off and tugged the door again.
Tugged it hard with both hands.
"Got to get OUT of here!"
I pushed it. I pulled it. I tugged with all my strength.
But I couldn't budge it.
I was trapped in the cage.
The door was jammed!

29

I felt a sharp stab of pain on the back of my neck.

It sent a cold chill that made my entire body shudder.

I reached one hand back and pulled a hamster off my neck. I set him down on the floor. Two more hamsters scrambled up my arm.

I let out a cry. I could feel them scratching and clawing on the back of my shirt.

I twisted my body. I squirmed and shook, trying to toss them off me.

But hamsters clung tightly to my shirt and my jeans. I heard a tearing sound as claws raked down my back.

I was hunched on my knees. I tugged at my shirt. They had *shredded* it!

Hamsters dug and clawed at my jeans pockets. I pulled another one from my hair.

"No more candy!" I shrieked. I felt another

sharp bite on my ankle. "No more candy! NO MORE!"

But they swarmed over me. Their claws raked my skin.

I tried the door again. Tugged with all my strength. But it wouldn't slide . . . wouldn't slide . . . wouldn't slide.

I need help, I told myself.

Hamsters covered my legs. I could feel them crawling *inside* my jeans!

Shaking them off, I dove to the glass cage wall.

Through the front window, I saw Lexi out on the sidewalk. Showing up for work.

"Lexi! HELP me!" I screamed through the glass. "HELP me! I need HELP!"

She waved and smiled at me through the store window. Then she turned her back on me. Who was she talking to? I recognized two girls from school.

"HELP ME!" I screamed at the top of my lungs. I pounded the cage wall with both fists. "Lexi! Can't you hear me?"

She didn't turn around. The two girls laughed about something. They kept on talking.

"Lexi! Help me!" I wailed.

Hamsters scraped the back of my neck. I could feel them rolling down my back. I let out a cry as a hamster bit my ear!

"Lexi! I need your help!"

I could see her right outside the shop door.

I pounded on the glass. I shouted some more.

Outside, the two girls laughed again and kept chattering away to Lexi. I saw Lexi wave to someone in a passing car.

"Lexi! Help me! Help me!"

I pounded the glass some more. Then I slid down to my knees, covered in hamsters.

I shoved them off my neck. I pulled two out of my hair.

I covered my head with my hands. But there was nowhere to hide, nowhere to escape.

The hamsters snarled and growled and kept up the attack. They swarmed over me. Two of them scratched and scraped at my jeans pockets.

"No more candy!" I cried. "No more!"

The hamsters tore frantically at my pockets. If I batted one away, another took its place.

I gasped as two hamsters ripped my jeans pocket completely off.

I stared in disbelief. The candy gave these hamsters amazing strength!

Then I noticed that something blue fell out of the missing pocket and hit the cage floor. It took me a few seconds to realize it was a couple of Insta-Gro Pets. The last two in the package.

I'd forgotten all about them.

What were they doing in there? Oh, yes. I'd stuffed them in there to keep them away from Noah.

Hamsters clung to my arms as I grabbed for them. Hamsters scratched my hair, crawled up my back.

Before I could pick them up, two hamsters raced from out of nowhere. They came hurtling out of a pile of wood shavings — and pounced on the little blue sponge animals.

"NOOOO!" I screamed. I made a wild grab for them.

Missed!

And then I stared in horror as one of the hamsters stuffed an Insta-Gro Pet into his mouth and began to chew.

30

"Nooooo!" I let out another hoarse scream as the hamster instantly started to grow.

In two seconds, he had ballooned to the size of a cat!

I grabbed for the second hamster. But another growling hamster leaped up and bit my hand.

Howling in pain, I toppled forward. I swung my throbbing hand out — and grabbed the second hamster. I pulled the Insta-Gro Pet from his paws.

I squeezed it tightly in my hand to keep it safe.

Hamsters scratched the back of my neck and nipped at my hair and scalp. Hamsters swarmed over my arms . . . my legs.

But I ignored them and stared at the growing hamster, bulging in front of me.

As big as a German shepherd now, he rose up on his hind legs. He scratched the air with enormous paws. Bigger . . . Bigger . . .

His belly bumped me hard — and sent me flying against the cage door.

The wire door unjammed. I quickly slid it open.

The hamster stretched . . . bobbed in front of me. Rose over me — at least *eight or ten feet tall* now.

His eyes were the size of tennis balls. His paws as big as baseball mitts!

And then, with a mighty heave, he shoved me out of his way and thundered to the open cage door.

And squeezed out of the cage.

He made a sick *plop* as his wide body hit the floor.

I froze in horror. The creature was *out*! The creature was FREE!

What would he do now?

He opened his jaws in a deafening roar. He flailed the air with his huge paws.

Then the hamster reached into the cage and GRABBED me.

"Huh?" I uttered a startled cry.

He dragged me out of the cage. Lifted me in the air as if I were as light as . . . as a HAMSTER!

"Let me down! Let me down!" My frantic cries were high and shrill.

I kicked my legs and tried to twist free.

But the enormous creature raised me high off the floor and dangled me in one paw.

"Lexi — help! HELP ME!" I screamed. "Lexi!!"

I could see her out the front door, talking to her friends. She didn't turn around.

"Lexi! I need HELLLLP!"

My scream cut off when the hamster swung me hard and slammed me into the wall.

Ooof. The air shot out of my body. I struggled to catch my breath.

Slam.

The giant hamster swung me hard into the wall again.

My head spun. Everything went bright yellow, then darkened to red.

SLAM.

I knew I couldn't take much more of this. A few more hits and I'd be out cold.

I suddenly remembered. I still had the last Insta-Gro Pet squeezed tightly in my hand.

SLAM.

I had no choice. I had to act fast. I had to fight this monster!

So . . . I slid the blue spongy thing into my mouth — and swallowed it down.

31

It tasted chalky. Like powder.

I swallowed once. Twice.

I let out a long burp. I could feel my stomach start to fizz and bubble.

I felt sick. I burped again, a long sour burp.

I heard a stretching sound. Like fabric ripping. My T-shirt went flying off me!

"Hey!" the shop began to move. The glass cage was rapidly shrinking!

No — wait. The *cage* wasn't changing. I was!

Yes. I was definitely stretching . . . growing longer . . . wider.

The big hamster dropped me. I hit the floor with a hard thud.

I climbed quickly to my feet. I bobbed unsteadily. I was so big, it was hard to catch my balance.

"WHOOOOAAAAA!" My cry came out in a deep, bellowing roar.

My toes ripped right through my sneakers. The top of my head was about to bang into the ceiling.

I was a *giant*!

Still growing?

I took a deep breath. No. I'd stopped.

Far below, my feet were enormous, poking out of my shredded sneakers.

I raised my eyes in time to see the giant hamster leap at me. We were the same size now. Both giants!

The hamster pressed his wide furry body against me and pushed hard.

Pushed me against the wall.

Pushed hard. His chest covered my face. I couldn't breathe.

He . . . he's trying to SMOTHER me! I realized.

I opened my mouth to take a breath — and swallowed fur.

Choking, I wrapped my long arms around the beast's middle and squeezed.

The hamster let out a whoosh of air.

I shoved him back. Turned my head and breathed. A long, deep breath.

He lowered his head and came at me. Head-butted me. A jarring blow.

Dazed, I tried to shake off the dizziness.

He head-butted me again. The creature was

panting loudly. His hot breath poured over me. He came at me again. My head throbbed. The room — so tiny ... so far below me ... It all began to spin.

I let out a choked gasp as the big creature's head bulled into my stomach.

I struggled to suck in air. But my chest burned like fire. My lungs weren't working right.

The hamster lowered his head. He was about to charge in for the kill.

One more head butt would finish me.

I saw him coming ... full speed.

He dove at me, head down.

And I *dodged* to the side.

CRAAAACK.

The hamster uttered a weak groan as his head slammed hard into the wall.

His black eyes rolled back in his head — and he fell on top of me.

I collapsed in a heap beneath him.

He covered me like a heavy blanket. I could hear the giant hamster wheezing above me.

He pressed his enormous body over me. Pressed down with all his massive weight.

Crushed me beneath him. Smothered me. Smothered me ...

32

My chest ached and throbbed. My lungs felt ready to explode.

With a last burst of strength, I pressed both hands on his massive chest — and pushed. *Pushed . . .*

I shoved the hulking creature off me and rolled on top of him. I straddled him with my legs.

He didn't fight back. He didn't try to get up.

I sucked in breath after breath. And suddenly felt the creature move beneath me.

"Yessss!" My cry came out weak but happy.

I knew what was happening. The monster hamster was shrinking. Shrinking back to his own size.

I remembered the Insta-Gro Pet on our dining room table. It stayed huge for only a few minutes.

And now the Insta-Gro Pet was wearing off. The hamster was shrinking.

He was the size of a dog now . . . the size of a squirrel . . . hamster size!

I sat up. Grabbed him — and lifted him between my two enormous fingers.

He snarled and tried to swipe his claws at me.

But I tossed him easily back into the open cage.

I climbed unsteadily to my feet. I still felt dizzy. I had to duck my head so it wouldn't hit the ceiling.

I took another breath. I could still feel the damp, hot fur of the giant hamster on my chest, smothering me.

"Ohhhh!" I uttered a cry as I felt myself start to fall.

So dizzy. I grabbed my head with both hands.

I bent my knees, struggling to stop from tumbling over.

What was happening?

The floor came flying up to meet me!

The whole shop was moving crazily. I shut my eyes, but I couldn't stop the dizzying rush.

My knees folded again. My legs quivered from side to side.

My body felt as if somebody had grabbed both ends and was squeezing me like an accordion!

But I didn't go down. I stayed on my feet as everything around me rose and fell.

It took me so long to realize that I was *shrinking*!

I heard a cracking sound. Was that my BONES?

My stomach heaved up into my throat. My legs bent and buckled.

A powerful force pressed down on me. I could feel my head sinking into my neck.

"Ohhhhh."

Did that moan come from *me*?

Still holding my head in both hands, I opened my eyes. I blinked several more times.

My arms and legs twitched. My feet were tucked back into my ripped shoes. My T-shirt lay in shreds on the floor.

But I was me again. The right size.

I hugged myself tightly, trying to stop my twitches and shakes. I was back. Back!

I heard an angry growl.

I glanced into the cage. Hamsters were growling and baring their teeth again.

The cage door was gone. They moved toward the opening.

I spotted a big sheet of wood against the wall. I grabbed it and leaned it against the cage opening.

"Thank goodness Fitz didn't see any of this!" I said out loud.

And then I heard footsteps on the basement stairs. And Mr. Fitz appeared in the doorway.

He stood there with his arms crossed in front of him. He looked at the cage. Then stared at me. Just stared, with the strangest expression on his face.

"Mr. Fitz, I can explain!" I cried. "I can explain everything. It was the candy! The candy!"

Finally, he moved. He stepped around the cage and came closer to me. He brushed his mustache with one hand as he stared at me.

"I can explain," I said. "It was the candy. I accidentally left my orange candy in the cage. They ate it all, Mr. Fitz. They ate all the candy. And it turned them mean!"

His eyes narrowed. I held my breath and waited for him to react.

I had ruined his hamsters, destroyed his shop. What was he going to do to me?

To my surprise, a smile crossed his face. "That was FABULOUS!" he cried. "I got the whole thing on video!"

33

I swallowed hard. "Excuse me?" I cried.

Fitz pointed to a tiny camera over the counter. "I got it all on video. That was *amazing*, Sam."

"But — but —" I sputtered. What was amazing? Why was he so *happy*?

I decided to try explaining to him again. "I'm so totally sorry about the candy," I said.

He laughed. His mustache bobbed up and down when he laughed.

"You got it wrong, Sam," he said. "It wasn't the candy."

I squinted at him. "Huh?"

"The candy didn't turn the hamsters mean," Fitz said. "It was the Vito-Vigor."

I opened my mouth but no sound came out. My brain was spinning. I struggled to understand what he was saying.

"The Vito-Vigor water is actually an *anger* drink I've been testing," Fitz said. "I've been giving it to them for weeks, waiting for it to work on them."

"You — you've been *trying* to turn the hamsters mean?" I stammered.

He nodded. "Not just mean," he said. "Vicious. I've been trying to turn them *ferocious!*"

I shook my head. "But why would anyone want to buy a ferocious hamster?"

Behind us, snarling hamsters threw themselves against the glass, trying to escape. Hamsters gnashed their teeth and clawed the cage wall.

"I've been waiting so long," Fitz said, watching the angry hamsters. "Waiting for the anger chemical to work on them."

He slapped me on the back. "This is a great day!" he cried. "Thank you, Sam. This is an important day!"

The slap stung my skin. My back was covered with hamster bites and scratches.

"I . . . I don't get it," I said. "Why do you want to take cute, cuddly hamsters and turn them vicious?" I asked again.

"A dozen reasons," Fitz said, grinning happily. "A dozen reasons — and they will all make me RICH!"

I waited for him to go on.

His grin grew wider. "Sam, can you imagine the excitement when I announce the WHWL?"

"The *what*?" I cried.

"The Worldwide Hamster Wrestling League," Fitz said. "People will jam stadiums and arenas to watch ferocious hamsters battle. I'll have TV contracts. All kinds of Angry Hamster T-shirts and jackets and caps and WHWL video games. It's going to be HUGE!"

"But, Mr. Fitz —" I started.

He clamped a hand over my mouth. "And what about watchdogs, Sam? You know, a lot of people can't afford to keep a dog. It's very expensive. So they'll want to buy a watch-hamster from me! A ferocious guard hamster to protect their houses!"

He jumped up and down. "A fortune! I'm going to make a fortune selling guard hamsters! And, Sam, what about the US Army?" he cried.

I took a step back. "The army?"

He poked me in the chest with one finger. "You don't think the military will be interested in fierce fighter hamsters? Of *course* they will! Hamster soldiers can go where no humans can go. I'll have whole squads of fighter hamsters in the army, Sam. Whole fighting squads! All mine! MINE!"

He's CRAZY! I told myself, taking another step back from him. *He's totally stark-raving NUTS!*

I grabbed the front door. "I . . . I've got to go," I said. I pulled the door open.

I took a step — and I felt his hand grab my shoulder and tug me back hard.

"Don't try to leave," Fitz said, his voice lowered to a growl. "You're not going anywhere, Sam."

34

He dragged me to the wall. His eyes burned into mine.

"Let me go," I said. "What do you want?"

"You're not going anywhere," Fitz said, "until you tell me the formula to make the hamster grow so enormous."

I swallowed. "Huh? Formula?"

"I can turn them mean," Fitz said. "But you know how to make them *gigantic.*"

He pressed me against the wall with both hands. "Tell me," he said. "Tell me how you did it. You're not going anywhere till you show me how to do it."

He was breathing noisily. His chest heaved up and down. Sweat ran down his face.

He's totally crazy, I thought. *I don't want to tell him about the Insta-Gro Pets. Besides, I don't have any left.*

"Tell me!" he insisted, his voice hoarse with excitement. "Tell me how you did it, Sam."

His eyes gleamed. "Can you imagine? An army of GIANT hamsters? Hundreds of them. As big as grown men? I could rule the WORLD with an army of giant hamsters! No one could defeat me! No one!"

"Mr. Fitz," I said softly, "you have to let me go."

"Not till you tell me the secret!" he cried. "I'll put you in the hamster cage, Sam. How would you like to spend some time in there?"

I gazed into the cage. Hamsters were snarling, snapping their jaws, frothing at the mouth.

"Tell me the secret!" Fitz screamed. "Or I'll put you in the cage!"

The bell jangled. The front door swung open. Lexi came bouncing in. "Hi, everyone!" she called.

Fitz turned to look at her.

That was my chance. I pulled free of his grasp. I dove to the cage — and pulled off the sheet of wood that covered the opening.

I tossed the wood away.

Growling hamsters came bursting out. They leaped to the floor and began running in all directions.

The front door was wide open. Two or three hamsters went darting out onto the sidewalk.

"No! Stop them! Catch them!" Fitz shrieked.

He began running in wild circles, pulling escaped hamsters up off the floor.

Lexi turned to me. "Any way I can help?" she asked.

"Help?" I cried. *"Help?* NOW you ask if you can help?"

Fitz was down on the floor, covered in growling, snapping hamsters.

I grabbed Lexi by the arm. "Let's go. We're out of here!"

She pulled back. "But — but —"

"I'll explain later!" I cried. "Hurry! This is our chance!"

We ran out of the shop. Ferocious, frothing hamsters were running up and down the street.

I heard Fitz yelling behind us. "Come back! Come back! I need the formula!"

Lexi and I took off running. We didn't stop till we were a block from her house.

We were both panting. I had a sharp pain in my side from running so hard.

"We made it!" I cried happily. "We made it out of there! What a nightmare! But it's over! It's OVER!"

Lexi mopped her forehead with her hand. "I'm so thirsty. I . . . wish I had a bottle of Vito-Vigor," she moaned.

"Oh, wow." I squinted at her. "Vito-Vigor? Lexi, how much of that stuff did you drink?"

She shrugged. "Just ten or twelve bottles. Why?"

I started to answer her.

But before I could utter a sound, Lexi opened her mouth in a hoarse cry. The cry became a bellowing roar.

She slashed her fingernails in the air, clawing furiously. Then she leaped high — and threw herself on me, scratching and growling — and sank her teeth deep into my neck!

EPILOGUE

35

I staggered home. The bite on my neck wasn't as bad as I thought. I covered it with a Band-Aid.

Of course, I was very worried about Lexi. I had pulled her to her house. But she kept clawing at me and trying to bite me.

Her parents had to keep her on a leash for a while. Luckily, the anger juice wore off in a day or two.

I slumped down on the edge of my bed. "I'll *never* get a pet now," I told myself. "But maybe I don't want one."

This whole hamster thing turned me off pets. Besides, why did I need a pet when Noah was around? He was a perfect pet!

I knew I had to change my clothes before my parents came home. I opened my closet door.

"Huh?" I let out a gasp of panic when I saw the glow of light from the floor.

Fire? Was my closet on fire?

No. The glow was soft and yellow-green.

I had dirty clothes strewn over the closet floor. I pulled away a shirt and a pair of cargo pants.

And stared at the little Horror the HorrorLand shopkeeper had attached to my souvenir box. The Horror was gleaming, a steady light.

I felt myself drawn to it. Pulled to it.

"Whoa!" I tried to push back in the other direction. I tried to propel myself out of the closet.

But the glowing Horror was like a powerful magnet. I couldn't resist it.

It pulled me closer . . . pulled me into the glowing yellow-green light. Pulled me . . . pulled hard.

The closet walls vanished. My room disappeared.

I sailed through the yellow-green glow. Sailed as if blown by a powerful wind. The glowing light formed soft tunnel walls. Soft and smooth.

Suddenly, the light flashed. And went out.

I felt myself land. My feet touched solid ground. I blinked in total darkness.

And then the lights went back on. I saw shelves of weird objects and souvenirs.

I knew where I was. I was back in HorrorLand. Back in that strange little shop. Chiller House.

And Jonathan Chiller stood at the counter, smiling at me. Jonathan Chiller in his old-fashioned suit and vest, gazing at me through those square eyeglasses perched on the end of his long nose.

"How — how did I get here?" I stammered.

His smile didn't change. "Welcome back, Sam," he said in his croaky old man's voice. His gold tooth gleamed.

"You remember my name?"

He nodded. "I hope you enjoyed your souvenirs," he said. His smile faded. "Now it's time for you to pay me back."

I felt a stab of fear run down my body. "Pay you back?"

"Time to pay me back for all the fun you've had with your Insta-Gro Pets," Chiller said.

"But I didn't have any fun!" I cried. "It was *horrifying!*"

Chiller's smile returned. "Don't worry, Sam. The fun is just BEGINNING."

He raised his eyes and gazed over my head. "But first . . . we have to wait for the others!"

HorrorLand TRADING CARDS

CHEF BELCHER

REAL NAME: Burr P. Belcher

HOMETOWN: Boils, Louisiana

SCHOOL: Roto Rooter Cooking Academy

PROUDEST ACHIEVEMENT:
Hasn't given anyone food poisoning since breakfast

HORRORLAND SPLAT STATS

HEAD LICE COUNT:	
NOSE HAIR LENGTH:	
SHOE SIZE (left):	
SHOE SIZE (right):	
SENSE OF SMELL:	
I.Q. COMPARED TO A DOG:	

The chef has been cooking up mischief since he was a young Belcher. On the playground he mixed a bowl of dirt and worms and told his friends it was "Chocolate Pudding Surprise." As a teenager, he fed his cat to his dog. He won the 2003 International Chef Award. Not for his cooking—for his projectile vomiting! Chef Belcher doesn't want to reveal his secret ingredient. He will only say: "It's something I find under my tongue."